Acting Edition

I0600483

Too Many Cooks

by Douglas Hughes
and Marcia Kash

‖SAMUEL FRENCH‖

TOO MANY COOKS premiered on July 23rd, 2003 at the Lighthouse Festival in Port Dover, Ontario. The performance was directed by Robert More, with sets by Jeff Johnston Collins, costumes by Ivan Brozik, and lighting by Wendy Greenwood. The Production Stage Manager was Beth Bruck. The cast was as follows:

IRVING BUBBALOWE........................... Michael Lamport

HONEY BUBBALOWE..............................Robin Schisler

FRANK PLUNKETT............................. Duncan Stewart

MICKEY McCALL................................. Peter Windrem

CONSTABLE HAMILTON X. EFFING.....................Steve Welch

ALFONSE FEGHETTI...............................Ralph Small

SHIRLEY... Oliver Becker

VERONICA SNOOK.................................Jill Harland

CHARACTERS

IRVING BUBBALOWE – Affable fellow in his mid-forties to mid-fifties. Proprietor of "Château Bubbalowe."

MICKEY McCALL – Scruffy-looking man in his forties. Delivery man for Dominion Warehouse.

HONEY BUBBALOWE – Attractive woman in her late twenties. Irving's daughter.

FRANK PLUNKETT – Pleasant-looking man in his thirties. Unemployed chef.

ALFONSE "NOODLES" FEGHETTI – Chicago mob boss, à la Al Capone. Mid-to-late forties.

SHIRLEY – Large, imposing mob enforcer type, mid-to-late thirties. Al's right-hand man.

VERONICA SNOOK – Officious-looking woman in her forties. Investigator for Canadian Immigration.

HAMILTON X. EFFING – Dudley Do-right type, in his mid-thirties to forties. Constable for the Royal Canadian Mounted Police.

(SETTING: The bar of "Le Château Bubbalowe," a small hotel in Niagara Falls, Ontario, in late spring, 1932. Downstage right is the bar. Against the stage right wall, upstage of the bar, is something that looks like a laundry chute which leads into the basement. A phone sits on the bar. Downstage of the bar, on the stage right wall, is a door leading to the basement. Upstage is an archway. Just left of the archway is a hall leading upstage to the main entrance of the hotel; off right we see the beginnings of a staircase leading to the rest of the hotel. Left of center on the upstage wall is a double set of swing doors leading to the kitchen. Upstage on the wall left is another set of double doors leading to the dining room. Although it is not apparent from this perspective, one can only go from the dining room to the kitchen through the bar. Downstage of the double doors on the left wall is a door leading into a large storage closet. Downstage left there is a small, round bar table, covered with a floor-length tablecloth. Around the table are two chairs. A suit jacket is draped over the back of one chair. This room is evidently not open to the public. There are no bottles behind the bar, for example, and there are a number of identical boxes of French Canadian pea soup stacked in two or three piles against the wall upstage center, with the name DOMINION WAREHOUSE stamped on them in large, bold letters, as well as other examples of restaurant paraphernalia here and there.)

*(AT RISE, we hear a recording of Pagliacci playing on a gramophone sitting on the bar. **IRVING BUBBALOWE**, the proprietor of the hotel, enters from the dining room, carrying a tuxedo on a hanger. He is an affable-looking man of medium build in his late forties, dressed in a shirt, tie and dress slacks with an apron overtop. **MICKEY MCCALL** enters from the basement. He is a*

8   TOO MANY COOKS

slightly scruffy-looking man in his forties. He's dressed in a cloth cap and overalls with the name "DOMINION WAREHOUSE" prominently displayed on the back. He is chewing gum and singing along with the record. He crosses to the pile of boxes and picks up a couple of them.)

MICKEY. *(singing along)* Ridi Pagliaccio – la la la la la la la

BUBBALOWE. What a voice, eh?

(He hangs the tuxedo on a hook on the wall behind the bar.)

MICKEY. Gee, thanks, Mr. Bubbalowe.

BUBBALOWE. No – I meant the record.

MICKEY. Oh. You know, maybe it's time to put on a different song. I mean, you've been playing that same record for the last half hour.

BUBBALOWE. I know, Mickey, but it's the only one I've got.

MICKEY. Well you better take it easy or it's going to wear out on you.

(The record begins to skip.)

What did I tell you?

BUBBALOWE. Darn it.

(He crosses to the gramophone and gives the needle a nudge. The song continues to its conclusion as he listens in ecstasy.)

What a talent!

MICKEY. Yeah, he's good, whoever he is. You know, I just love opera.

BUBBALOWE. Then you're in luck. You're going to be hearing a lot of it around here from now on.

MICKEY. I am?

BUBBALOWE. Haven't you heard who's going to be running my kitchen?

MICKEY. Who?

BUBBALOWE. The Maestro himself – François LaPlouffe!

MICKEY. François LaPlouffe? Never heard of him.

BUBBALOWE. You've never heard of François LaPlouffe? And you call yourself an opera buff. He's a world-famous tenor. That was him we were just listening to.

MICKEY. I'm confused – you hired a tenor to run your kitchen?

BUBBALOWE. He's not just a tenor. He's also a world-famous chef.

MICKEY. No kiddin'. Can he cook as well as he can sing?

BUBBALOWE. You bet he can. They don't call him "Maestro" for nothing. He's worked in some of the finest restaurants in the world.

MICKEY. Imagine that. How did you get a guy like that to come and work here in Niagara Falls?

BUBBALOWE. It was all Honey's doing. She stole him away from the Royal York Hotel in Toronto.

MICKEY. The Royal York, eh? How'd she manage that?

BUBBALOWE. Oh, you don't know my daughter – when she sets her sights on something, she usually gets it. I'm telling you Mickey, LaPlouffe is going to put this place on the map. When word gets out about him, those honeymooners will be coming to Niagara Falls with only one thing on their minds – okay, two things. But one of them will be eating in my restaurant.

MICKEY. So when does he get here?

BUBBALOWE. *(looking at his watch)* Any minute now. Honey's just gone down to the train station to meet him.

MICKEY. *(pulling out a cigarette case and offering one to* **BUBBALOWE***)* Smoke?

BUBBALOWE. No thanks. Those things'll kill you, you know.

MICKEY. *(putting the case away)* Maybe you're right. I should try to cut down. I'll tell you somethin' though, Mr. Bubbalowe – you got a lot of guts, opening a restaurant in the middle of this depression. Do you know how many places I seen go under in the last three years? The only guys that have managed to survive are the ones shippin' booze over the border for the Americans.

BUBBALOWE. Well, there won't be any of that nonsense going on here. My Aunt Agatha ran this place for thirty years. She saw it through worse times than these, and she never had to resort to rum running. If she could do it, then so can I!

MICKEY. I'm glad to hear you say that, Mr. Bubbalowe. I wish more people in this town felt that way. Ever since those Yanks came up with Prohibition, everyone in Niagara Falls has turned into a crook.

BUBBALOWE. Everyone but me. I'm going to make this place a success the honest way. Besides, I've got something none of those other guys have – I've got François LaPlouffe. With him in my restaurant I'm going to make a fortune. Oh, and speaking of fortunes, *(handing* **MICKEY** *a wad of bills)* here's what I owe you.

MICKEY. Thanks. I'm just gonna finish up with these boxes, and I'll be on my way.

BUBBALOWE. Are you sure you don't want any help?

MICKEY. No, no, really, Mr. Bubbalowe, it's okay. I'm nearly done anyway.

BUBBALOWE. Well, then let me at least give you a little something for your trouble.

(With a sigh, he hands **MICKEY** *one last bill.)*

MICKEY. Gee, thanks Mr. Bubbalowe!

*(***MICKEY*** *pockets the bill and picks up a couple of boxes.* **BUBBALOWE** *notices the label.)*

BUBBALOWE. French Canadian Pea Soup? I don't remember ordering any of that.

MICKEY. *(chuckling)* Hey, knowing those numbskulls in shipping and receiving, there's a good chance you didn't. But you know how it works – if it's on the invoice, I gotta deliver it. Listen, don't worry about it. I'll double--check the order when I get back to the warehouse. If it's a mistake, I'll have somebody pick this stuff up tomorrow and we'll get it outta your hair.

BUBBALOWE. OK, fair enough.

(BUBBALOWE exits into the kitchen. MICKEY looks around to see the coast is clear. He opens a box of the "pea soup.")

MICKEY. *(mimicking BUBBALOWE)* "There won't be any of that nonsense going on here." Geez, what a chump!

(He pulls out a bottle of whiskey.)

You're not the only one who's gonna be makin' a fortune, Bubbalowe!

(He cackles with delight, gives the bottle a kiss, and puts it back in the box. He picks up some boxes and starts to exit into the basement.)

(singing along with the record) La-la-la-la-la.

(HONEY BUBBALOWE, an attractive young woman in her mid- to late twenties, enters from the archway, wearing a hat and carrying a chef's hat and a large book.)

HONEY. Pop?

BUBBALOWE. *(off)* Coming!

(She crosses to the bar and puts down the hat and book. BUBBALOWE bustles in from the kitchen, straightening his tie.)

Monsieur LaPlouffe! Bienvenue au Château – *(stops in his tracks)* Where is he?

HONEY. *(taking off her hat and setting down her purse)* He wasn't on the train.

BUBBALOWE. What do you mean he wasn't on the train?

HONEY. The only people who got off were a dozen members of the Elora Ladies' Lawn Bowling League.

BUBBALOWE. Maybe you just missed him.

HONEY. Not unless he was dressed in a white skirt and matching shoes.

BUBBALOWE. Well what do you suppose happened to him?

HONEY. I don't know, but the conductor found these on one of the seats.

(She holds up the chef's hat and the book.)

His recipe book and his hat.

BUBBALOWE. *(looking in the hat)* Well where's the rest of him?

HONEY. I don't know.

BUBBALOWE. What? Why would his things be on the train if he wasn't? *(a sudden thought)* Maybe he's been kidnapped!

HONEY. Now Pop, don't be silly! I'm sure there's a very simple explanation. He probably just went to buy a magazine or something and the train pulled out of the station without him.

BUBBALOWE. Well if that's what happened, why didn't he just phone and tell us?

HONEY. Look, Pop, there's another train in a couple of hours. Why don't we wait and see if he's on it?

BUBBALOWE. Honey, we don't have a couple of hours. We're short of time as it is. I knew we should have talked him into getting here yesterday.

HONEY. We'll be fine, Pop. All we have to do is make sure that everything's ready for him when he gets here. Now why don't you go down to Bucky's and pick up the geese, and I'll get things going here.

BUBBALOWE. *(a sudden realization)* What if he doesn't show up at all?

HONEY. Now, Pop...

BUBBALOWE. *(as panic begins to set in)* We've got sixty guests coming here tonight for this gala opening. They're expecting a gourmet meal, served by François LaPlouffe the famous singing chef! Instead they're going to be treated to an evening of canned pea soup and Irving Bubbalowe's famous record collection!

HONEY. What famous collection? You've only got one record.

BUBBALOWE. Well at least it'll be a short evening. Oh my God, this is going to be a disaster.

HONEY. Calm down.

BUBBALOWE. Calm down? How do you expect me to calm down? I'm opening a restaurant and I have no chef! *(holding up the book and hat)* LaPluff's vanished in a pouffe of smoke.

HONEY. Come on Pop –

BUBBALOWE. I should have known better than to trust a Frenchman. We're going to be out of business before we've even opened.

HONEY. Now don't say that –

BUBBALOWE. I just gave Mickey the last of our cash, you know. We're now officially broke. We've spent every penny Aunt Agatha left us on renovating this place. We would have done better to sell it and split the money.

HONEY. *(crossing to the kitchen doors)* Now Pop, don't panic. It'll all work out.

BUBBALOWE. Not without François LaPlouffe, it won't.

HONEY. Well look at it this way: at least we've got all his recipes. If worse comes to worst, we can hire someone else to cook the dinner.

(She exits into the kitchen.)

BUBBALOWE. Oh, sure. Singing chefs are a dime a dozen. Any minute now, another will just come walking in that door!

*(He follows her into the kitchen. **FRANK PLUNKETT** enters. He's a nice-looking man in his thirties, wearing a shabby suit and carrying a suitcase with his name printed on the side in large letters.)*

FRANK. Hello-o?

*(He sets down the suitcase as **MICKEY** enters from the basement.)*

Oh! *(tidying himself up a bit)* Good morning. Are you the owner?

MICKEY. No that'd be Mr. Bubbalowe. You must be the new chef.

FRANK. Well, I sure hope to be. *(offering his hand)* The name's Plunkett. Frankie Plunkett.

MICKEY. Plunkett? Oh no, sorry, I thought you were somebody else.

FRANK. You mean they've already got a chef?

MICKEY. Afraid so.

FRANK. *(dejectedly)* Oh. I was hoping they might be hiring.

MICKEY. You'd have to talk to Mr. Bubbalowe about that.

FRANK. I'd take just about anything at this point. I've been from one end of this country to the other, and I can't find a job anywhere.

MICKEY. Lot of that going around these days.

(He exits into the basement with a couple more boxes. **FRANK** *looks around, spots the chef's hat on the bar. He picks it up wistfully and puts it on his head. He picks up the recipe book just as* **BUBBALOWE** *enters, calling over his shoulder.)*

BUBBALOWE. *(crossing downstage left to get his jacket)* I'll be back in five minutes. Keep an eye out for our vanishing Frenchman.

(He turns, sees **FRANK**, *and jumps.)*

Aagh! *(registering the chef's hat and recipe book)* Oh you made it after all! Thank goodness!

FRANK. Huh?

BUBBALOWE. *(clearing his throat in preparation)* Bienvenue au Château Bubbalowe, Monsieur. Ç'est un grand honneur de faire votre connaîssance!

*(***BUBBALOWE** *bows deeply.* **FRANK**, *flummoxed, bows in response.)*

That's about the extent of my French, I'm afraid. I've been practising for days. Anyway, I'm glad you managed to find your way here. Honey must have just missed you at the station. Oh, my goodness – where are my manners? *(offering his hand)* Irving Bubbalowe, at your service.

FRANK. But Mr. Bubbalowe –

BUBBALOWE. *(pumping his hand)* Please, call me Irving. And may I say how honoured we are that you've chosen to come and work with us. You have no idea how much this means to us.

FRANK. But sir, I'm not –

BUBBALOWE. Oh, there's no need to be modest with me, Monsieur LaPlouffe. I've been a fan of yours for years.

FRANK. LaPlouffe?

BUBBALOWE. Or would you prefer I called you Maestro?

FRANK. Maestro?

BUBBALOWE. Fine. Maestro it is.

FRANK. But –

BUBBALOWE. You know, you don't look anything like I pictured you. I imagined you'd be – larger, somehow.

FRANK. Well –

BUBBALOWE. *(indicating the recipe book and hat)* I see you've found your things. Listen, the kitchen's right over here. You go ahead and make yourself at home. *(taking off the apron and putting on his jacket)* I'll be right back. I'm just on my way to go and pick up the geese.

FRANK. Geese?

BUBBALOWE. For your famous Goose Gallantine! I can't wait to try it. *(shaking his hand again)* Gee, it's great to have you here! With you in my kitchen, I just know this place is going to be a gold mine!

(He crosses to the archway.)

Oh – and any time you'd like to warm up, there's a piano in the dining room.

*(**BUBBALOWE** exits.)*

FRANK. Piano?

*(**HONEY** enters from the kitchen, wearing an apron and carrying a bowl of punch. **FRANK** stands there, instantly smitten.)*

HONEY. Pop – where's the – oh, hello. Who are you?

FRANK. Uh, the chef.

HONEY. Chef?

FRANK. Maestro?

HONEY. Maestro?

FRANK. Monsieur LaPlouffe?

HONEY. What are you talking about? You're not François LaPlouffe.

FRANK. I'm not?

HONEY. *(setting the punch bowl on the table downstage right)* No. I met him in Toronto two weeks ago, and you're definitely not him. Now, what are you trying to pull?

FRANK. Nothing, Miss, I just –

HONEY. What's your name?

FRANK. Frankie Plunkett.

HONEY. *(frostily)* Well, Mr. Plunkett, would you mind telling me what you're doing here?

FRANK. I'm not really sure.

HONEY. I beg your pardon?

FRANK. I just came here looking for a job. The owner seemed to think I was this LaPlouffe character and he disappeared before I had a chance to tell him otherwise.

HONEY. I see. So you thought you'd just take Monsieur LaPlouffe's place, is that it? And how long were you planning on keeping up this charade?

FRANK. I don't know. I guess I wasn't thinking things through. I've been so desperate – I haven't worked in over a year… I mean, it wouldn't be so bad if I only had myself to worry about, but my Mom's been sick, you see, and I haven't been able to send her any money for a long time now. Look, I'm awfully sorry. I didn't mean to…uh, I think I'll just be on my way.

(He picks up his suitcase and turns to go.)

HONEY. *(touched by his story)* Mr. Plunkett?

FRANK. Yes?

HONEY. I'm sorry about your troubles, I really am. I wish there were something I could do to help you.

FRANK. Thanks Miss, I appreciate that. Goodbye, now.

HONEY. Goodbye.

(FRANK exits through the archway. She watches him go, wistfully. The phone rings.)

HONEY. *(picking up the phone)* Château Bubbalowe... Yes, operator, this is Honey Bubbalowe...from whom?... *(excited)* Yes, I'll take the call... Monsieur LaPlouffe? Where are you?... I beg your pardon?...

(FRANK re-enters, unseen by her.)

What do you mean you're not coming?... Going back to France!?... But what about our agreement? We've got our big opening tonight... What was that?... Who's after you?... Monsieur LaPlouffe? *(jiggling the telephone hook)* Monsieur LaPlouffe? Hello?

(She puts her head in her hands.)

FRANK. *(taking the chef's hat off his head)* Er, excuse me Miss, I think this belongs to you.

(He hands her the hat.)

HONEY. *(gruffly)* Thank you.

(She takes the hat and, with a growl, begins strangling it.)

FRANK. Pardon me, but I couldn't help overhearing – did you say your chef wasn't coming?

HONEY. That's right. He's left the country – and left us in the lurch! It's our grand opening tonight, and we have no one to cook the dinner!

FRANK. Well, it seems we might be able to help each other after all.

HONEY. What do you mean?

FRANK. *I* can cook your dinner.

HONEY. You?

FRANK. That's right. I may not be LaPlouffe, but I am a chef.

HONEY. A chef?

> *(suspicious)* Wait a minute. You're not just saying that to get a job, are you?

FRANK. No, I'm a chef, honest! Here – here's my card.

> *(He pulls a business card out of his pocket and hands it to her.)*

HONEY. *(reading)* Frank Plunkett, Chef de Maison… *(incredulous)* Max*im's*? *(giving it the French pronunciation)* You were a chef at Maxim's?

FRANK. That's right.

HONEY. *(excitedly)* Maxim's in Paris, France?

FRANK. No, Maxim's *(MACK-sims)* in Regina, Saskatchewan.

HONEY. *(crestfallen)* Oh. *(decisively)* Never mind. It'll do. Mr. Plunkett, you're hired.

> *(She plunks the chef's hat back on his head and shoves his card in his pocket.)*

FRANK. *(thrilled)* Really?

HONEY. Really.

FRANK. *(offering his hand)* Why, thank you! You don't know how much I appreciate this, Miss – er –

HONEY. *(taking his hand)* Bubbalowe. Honey Bubbalowe.

FRANK. Oh, the boss's daughter, eh? *(pumping her hand)* Well, it sure is a pleasure to meet you, Miss Bubbalowe and I promise I'll do a good job for you. Now, where should I start?

> *(He turns toward the kitchen.)*

HONEY. Just a moment, Mr. Plunkett. There is just one thing.

FRANK. What's that?

HONEY. We can't tell my father who you really are.

FRANK. Why not?

HONEY. Because he's banked the success of this place on LaPlouffe's name. If Pop finds out that his François LaPlouffe is really Frank Plunkett, this restaurant of ours will never open, and you'll be out of a job.

FRANK. Oh Miss Bubbalowe, I don't think I –

HONEY. Look, Pop already thinks you're LaPlouffe anyway
– all you have to do is keep on pretending to be him!

*(**HONEY** crosses to the closet, opens the door. Inside there
are several shelves on which are stocked linens, chef's
whites, canned goods etc.)*

FRANK. But I can't do that! I don't even speak French!

HONEY. *(crossing to him with an armful of chef's whites)* You
won't have to. Just put on an accent.

FRANK. What?

HONEY. You know – *(putting on a strong Francophone accent,
talking out of the side of her mouth)* talk like dat! Now
here –

(She hands him the whites.)

FRANK. Yes, but what am I supposed to cook? I don't know
any of LaPlouffe's recipes.

HONEY. *(handing him the recipe book)* They're all in here. Now –
(handing him the menu) here's this evening's menu.
Everything else you need is in the kitchen.

FRANK. But if your Dad finds out who I really am –

HONEY. Look, Mr. Plunkett, all you have to do is get
through tonight. Believe me, if the opening is a success, Pop will be so grateful to you, he won't care if
you're – Betty Boop!

FRANK. I don't feel right about this, Miss Bubbalowe. It's
dishonest.

HONEY. Please, Frank, you're our only hope. We can't open
this restaurant without François LaPlouffe – *(taking his
hand)* in other words, without *you.*

FRANK. *(crumbling)* Oh, alright.

HONEY. Oh, thank you!

*(She kisses him on the cheek. **FRANK** has to steady himself to keep from swooning. **HONEY** heads toward the
dining room.)*

Now, you'd better get started. We're way behind. I'll
be right here in the dining room if you need anything.

FRANK. I don't know if I can pull this off –

HONEY. You'll do fine, Mr. Plunkett. I have every confidence in you.

(beat)

As long as Pop doesn't ask you to sing…

(She exits into the dining room.)

FRANK. Sing?

*(He exits into the kitchen. **BUBBALOWE** enters through the archway struggling with two heavy sacks as **MICKEY** enters from the basement.)*

BUBBALOWE. Hey Mickey, did you see my neon sign out front?

MICKEY. How could I miss it? It's gotta be the biggest thing this side of the Falls! They'll be able to see it all the way from Bubbalowe, Mr. Buffalo – er, Buffalo, Mr. Bubbalowe. What's in the bags?

BUBBALOWE. Geese. *(setting them down)* Oof! Very well-fed geese.

MICKEY. You got someone to cook 'em for you yet?

BUBBALOWE. Yes, LaPlouffe's arrived, thank goodness. *(spotting **FRANK**'s suitcase)* Hey! Where did this come from? *(reading the name on the side of the case)* Frank Plunkett? Who the heck is he?

MICKEY. Plunkett? Oh, just some hobo – he was here looking for a job. He must have forgot it.

BUBBALOWE. *(putting it down near the bar)* Oh, well. I'll leave it here in case he comes back.

*(**MICKEY** picks up a couple more boxes.)*

Here, Mickey. Let me give you a hand with those.

MICKEY. *(as **BUBBALOWE** moves to pick up a couple of boxes)* No no, that's OK, Mr. Bubbalowe. You don't have to –

BUBBALOWE. *(picking up the boxes and jiggling them)* That's odd. Do you hear that?

MICKEY. Hear what?

BUBBALOWE. I thought this was canned pea soup. *(jiggling them again)* Sounds more like bottles to me.

(He sets down the boxes.)

MICKEY. It's probably just ketchup or somethin.' They label these boxes wrong all the time.

BUBBALOWE. I don't remember ordering ketchup, either.

(He starts to open a box.)

MICKEY. Don't do that, Mr. Bubbalowe!

BUBBALOWE. Hey, take it easy! I just want to see what this is. *(pulling a bottle of whiskey out of the box)* What the heck – whiskey?

MICKEY. Whoa! How did that get in there?

BUBBALOWE. Why don't you tell me?

MICKEY. How should I know?

BUBBALOWE. *(suspicious)* What's going on here, Mickey?

MICKEY. I don't know, er, there must have been some kinda mistake.

BUBBALOWE. Mistake? How does a box of pea soup get loaded up with whiskey by mistake? *(as the penny drops)* Wait a minute – *(He opens another box, and pulls out another bottle of whiskey.)*

Oh my God. How many of these 'mistakes' did you bring me?

MICKEY. Er....five hundred?

BUBBALOWE. FIVE HUNDRED?!! You mean I've got five hundred cases of bootleg booze in my basement?

MICKEY. That's about the size of it, yeah.

BUBBALOWE. What are you doing, bringing this stuff here? Do you realize what'll happen to me if I get caught with it? They'll shut me down – I'll be ruined! You've got to get it out of here now, before anybody sees it.

(HONEY enters. BUBBALOWE hides the bottles behind his back.)

HONEY. Anything wrong, Pop?

BUBBALOWE. Wrong? No, no. What could be wrong? Ha ha ha!!

(**FRANK** *enters from the kitchen, now dressed in chef's whites.*)

Ah, Maestro! What can I do for you?

FRANK. Excuse me, Mr – *(launching into a bad French accent)* uh, Monsieur Bubbaloo, I'm ready to start zee mousse, but zee salmon, I cannot find 'er.

HONEY. *(crossing to get her coat and purse)* Oh, the salmon! I forgot to pick it up this morning. I'll be right back.

FRANK. *(panicked, as she heads for the archway)* But Meess Bubbaloo, you cannot leave, I –

HONEY. Don't worry Monsieur LaPlouffe, it's just around the corner. Back in a jiffy.

(*She exits through the archway.* **BUBBALOWE** *shoves the bottles into* **MICKEY***'s hands, crosses to the bags of geese.*)

BUBBALOWE. I'm so sorry about that Maestro, but the good news is I've got your geese!

FRANK. Huh? I mean uh, honh?

BUBBALOWE. A dozen Grade-A grain fed birds, just as you requested.

(*He picks up the geese and hands them to* **FRANK**, *who looks at them trepidatiously.*)

FRANK. Ah, oui. I weel start on zose toute de suite. Merçi, Monsieur.

MICKEY. *(recognizing* **FRANK***)* Hey, it's Frankie, ain't it?

FRANK. *(panicked)* Huh?

BUBBALOWE. *(indignantly)* That's François to you, you ignoramus!

FRANK. Please excuse me, but like zee geese, I must fly!

(*He dashes into the kitchen.* **BUBBALOWE** *wheels on* **MICKEY** *and grabs his collar.*)

BUBBALOWE. Alright you little weasel. Now get this stuff out of here!

MICKEY. Hey, take it easy, Mr. Bubbalowe!

BUBBALOWE. Take it easy? You fill my basement with five hundred cases of contraband liquor and you expect me to take it easy? You're lucky I don't take your head off! Now, who does this stuff belong to – you?

MICKEY. Well, not exactly.

BUBBALOWE. Then who does it belong to, 'exactly'?

MICKEY. Uh…Alfonse Feghetti.

BUBBALOWE. Alfonse Feghetti? *(releasing him)* You mean Noodles Feghetti – the Chicago gangster?

MICKEY. That's right.

BUBBALOWE. How did you get mixed up with Noodles Feghetti?

MICKEY. Didn't you know? He's been shippin' booze through Dominion Warehouse for years.

BUBBALOWE. He has?

MICKEY. Sure. That's how he gets it over the border. We pack it in our boxes and drive it across in our trucks.

(He replaces the bottles in the boxes and closes them up.)

BUBBALOWE. You mean to tell me you work for Noodles Feghetti?

MICKEY. Well I did. Until today.

BUBBALOWE. What do you mean?

MICKEY. I'm sick and tired of breakin' my back for slave wages while Feghetti sits in Chicago rakin' in all the dough. I'm gettin' outta this racket, and this – *(indicating boxes)* is my ticket.

BUBBALOWE. You stole five hundred cases of booze from Noodles Feghetti? He's going to kill you!

MICKEY. I'm not stealin' a thing. This shipment's gonna get 'hijacked' by Morris the Hound.

BUBBALOWE. Morris "the Hound" Berger?

MICKEY. That's right. He's comin' to pick it up today. Gave me a real good price for it too. He's been itchin' to cut into Al's liquor business for ages.

BUBBALOWE. But Feghetti's going to know that somebody at the warehouse tipped off Morris the Hound. He'll find you.

MICKEY. No he won't. By the time he figures out who it was I'll be long gone.

BUBBALOWE. But why bring it here? What does any of this have to do with me?

MICKEY. I needed somewhere to stash the stuff until Morris the Hound could pick it up – somewhere Feghetti didn't know about. Everything was goin' along fine, too, till you started gettin' nosey.

BUBBALOWE. It's a good thing I did.

(**BUBBALOWE** *crosses to the phone.*)

MICKEY. Hey, what are you doing?

BUBBALOWE. I'm calling the police.

MICKEY. I wouldn't do that if I were you.

BUBBALOWE. Why not?

MICKEY. You'll only make it worse for yourself.

BUBBALOWE. What are you talking about?

MICKEY. Alright – go ahead and call them if you want; but what are you gonna tell 'em?

BUBBALOWE. The truth.

MICKEY. What – that you just let me load five hundred cases of Noodles Feghetti's booze into your basement without knowing about it? They're gonna think you're in on it, Bubbalowe.

BUBBALOWE. Nonsense. They'll believe me.

(*He picks up the phone.* **MICKEY** *pushes the hook down with his finger.*)

MICKEY. Even if they do, you know what'll happen then? You're goin' to have Morris the Hound *and* Noodles Feghetti after you for handin' their booze over to the cops – and believe you me, that's not somethin' you want.

BUBBALOWE. Morris the Hound and Noodles Feghetti – after ME?

(MICKEY takes the phone from BUBBALOWE and sets it back on the hook.)

MICKEY. Look Mr. Bubbalowe, there's an easy way out of this. All you gotta do is keep your mouth shut till Morris gets here, and I'll make it worth your while. Tell you what, I'll give you ten percent of my cut, right off the top. Here –

(He pulls out the wad of bills BUBBALOWE gave him earlier.)

MICKEY. You can even have an advance.

(BUBBALOWE looks down at the money. Beat.)

BUBBALOWE. I'll take my chances with the police.

(He reaches for the phone.)

MICKEY. Alright, Bubbalowe, if you want to do it the hard way –

(MICKEY pulls out a gun and aims it at BUBBALOWE.)

Hands up. Step away from the telephone.

BUBBALOWE. *(setting the phone down and raising his arms)* Mickey! What are you doing?

MICKEY. *(hanging up the phone)* Shut up. I'm the one giving the orders now. Pick up those boxes and take 'em downstairs.

(BUBBALOWE picks up a couple of boxes.)

BUBBALOWE. What are you going to do, kill me?

MICKEY. Don't worry, Bubbalowe. As long as you do as you're told, nobody'll get hurt. But remember – you say one word to anyone, *(indicating the restaurant)* and you can kiss all of this goodbye. Now move it.

(BUBBALOWE exits down the stairs. MICKEY follows him and shuts the door. Two boxes still remain. As the basement door closes, ALFONSE FEGHETTI enters through the archway upstage. AL is a typical mob boss type in his mid-forties, dressed in the appropriate garb and chewing on a large, unlit cigar. However, he carries his head tilted to one side, obviously in some discomfort.

SHIRLEY, his lieutenant, follows him on. SHIRLEY is a large, imposing enforcer type in his mid-to-late thirties.)

AL. *(rubbing his neck)* Jeez, my neck is killin' me. Who did Guido think he was makin' that coffin for, Mickey Rooney? Thanks to him, I'm gonna be walkin' around like this for the rest of my life.

SHIRLEY. Still, it got you over the border, didn't it? I told you those pansies at customs would be too chicken to inspect a stiff.

AL. May-be. But another few miles in that box and you woulda had a real stiff on your hands. *(rubbing his neck again)* Son-of-a-bitch! How am I supposed to do business like this?

(SHIRLEY crosses to him.)

SHIRLEY. Here. Hold still.

(He grabs AL on either side of the head and with one sharp motion, adjusts his neck back to normal.)

AL. AAGGH!

(pulling his gun on SHIRLEY, then discovering that he actually feels better)

Ah. That's better. Thanks, Shirley.

SHIRLEY. Don't mention it, Boss.

AL. *(putting his gun away)* You know, I'm gettin' too old to go round riskin' my neck like this.

SHIRLEY. What you need is a good massoose.

AL. Massoose, nothin.' I'll tell you what I need – I need a vacation. I'm tired of this nonsense – chasin' after punks like this Mickey McCall. Can you believe the nerve of that little rat, thinkin' he could double-cross Alfonse Feghetti? In the old days, this never woulda happened. You know what it is, Shirl? I'm gettin' soft. I'm losin' my touch. Maybe it's time I retired.

SHIRLEY. Retired? You? You gotta be kiddin.' What would you do all day if you retired?

AL. Start livin', for one thing. God knows I got enough scratch – I just never have the time to enjoy it. Do you realize how long it's been since I had a day off? I'm tellin' you, Shirl, I woulda retired years ago, 'cept for I could never find the right girl to settle down with.

SHIRLEY. What are you talkin' about? You got dames comin' out of the woodwork!

AL. Yeah, but I don't mean some cheap floozy; I mean somebody to come home to. Somebody special – somebody who can really appreciate me for who I am.

SHIRLEY. Don't worry, Boss. It'll happen one day. Good-lookin' fella like you?

AL. Shaddup. You're startin' to sound like my mother.

(looking around)

You sure this is the right place?

SHIRLEY. *(opening the chute)* Must be. Look at this – a bottle drop.

(He takes a coin from his pocket and tosses it down. A beat and then we hear it land down in the basement.)

Just like one of your speaks back home.

*(**AL** spots the boxes of pea soup.)*

AL. Hey, lookie here! French Canadian pea soup.

(He opens up the box and pulls out a bottle.)

Bingo!

SHIRLEY. Looks like your snitch knew what he was talkin' about.

*(**VERONICA SNOOK** enters from upstage. She is an officious-looking woman in her forties, wearing a dress and raincoat and carrying a briefcase.)*

VERONICA. Excuse me.

*(**AL** tosses the bottle to **SHIRLEY**, who hides it behind his back. He and **SHIRLEY** smile innocently.)*

AL. Yes, Ma'am.

VERONICA. Uh – hello. Are you Mr. Bubbalowe?

AL. *(appreciating her legs)* Who wants to know?

VERONICA. My name's Snook. Veronica Snook. My card.

(She pulls out a card and gives it to **AL.***)*

AL. Pleased to meet you – Mrs. Shnook?

VERONICA. That's Miss, actually. And it's Snook. Without the shnuh.

AL. *(beaming)* Charmed, I'm sure.

VERONICA. And you are?

AL. Call me Al.

VERONICA. Well – Al, perhaps you could help me. I'm looking for a François LaPlouffe.

AL. LaPoof? You mean that singin' chef?

VERONICA. That's right.

SHIRLEY. Sorry, lady. We ain't seen nobody like that.

AL. Wish we could help. Uh, if this Francoise LaPoof shows up, you want I should give him a message?

VERONICA. No, that's alright. I'll check back later.

SHIRLEY. Good idea.

AL. Hey, what's your hurry? Sit down, take a load off.

SHIRLEY. *(warning him)* Boss!

VERONICA. That's very kind of you, but I really must be going.

AL. Gee, that's too bad. Listen, you come and see us again real soon, OK?

VERONICA. *(smiling)* Oh I'll be back. You have my word on it.

AL. We'll be lookin' forward to it.

*(***VERONICA** *exits upstage.)*

Shirl, did you get a load of that dame?

SHIRLEY. Now, Boss –

AL. *(looking off through the archway)* I think she likes me!

SHIRLEY. Boss, this ain't the time.

(*setting the bottle on the bar and taking* **VERONICA**'s *card from* **AL**)

Now come on, we got work to do – holy smoke. Look at this! (*showing him the card*) "Government of Canada." She's a Fed!

AL. (*titillated*) No kiddin'? I ain't never seen a lady cop before.

SHIRLEY. (*putting card down on the bar*) Lady cops? That ain't natural.

AL. Seems like a pretty good idea to me.

SHIRLEY. It's un-American, that's what it is. Lady cops. Imagine that. These Canucks sure play by different rules.

AL. Yeah, ain't it great?

SHIRLEY. Come on, Boss. Let's get movin.' We gotta get that booze across the border before Morris the Hound shows up. We don't want a shootout here or we'll have Miss Shnook and her buddies swarmin' all over us.

AL. She can swarm all over me any time she wants to. Anyways, we ain't goin' nowhere till I get my hands on that fink Mickey. I'm gonna carve him up like a Thanksgiving turkey. Then I'm gonna go over to that warehouse of his and burn it to the ground.

SHIRLEY. Now Boss, we don't need to be here for that. The boys'll look after it.

AL. Look, I came here to take care of things personally. I'm gonna show these monkeys what happens when you try and make a chump outta Alphonse Feghetti.

(**MICKEY** *enters from the basement and closes the door. He sees* **AL** *and* **SHIRLEY** *and freezes in his tracks.*)

Well, look who's here, Shirl.

MICKEY. Mr. Feghetti! What are you doing here?

AL. I was about to ask you the same question. Frisk him, Shirley.

(**SHIRLEY** *begins to frisk him.*)

MICKEY. Look, Mr. Feghetti, I can explain –

AL. What's to explain? You stole my booze, now you're gonna pay for it.

SHIRLEY. *(pulling out Mickey's gun)* What's this for, Mickey? Target practice?

MICKEY. No, protection!

AL. Protection, huh? From who – me?

MICKEY. No, Mr. Feghetti – from, from – Bubbalowe!

AL. Bubbalowe? Who's Bubbalowe?

MICKEY. Irving Bubbalowe. The owner of this joint. It was all his idea. He made me do it!

AL. Oh yeah?

MICKEY. He said he was gonna kill me if I didn't go along with it. I didn't want to Mr. Feghetti, but –

(**SHIRLEY** *pulls the wad of cash from Mickey's pocket and waves it in his face.*)

SHIRLEY. But he talked you into it, right?

MICKEY. No, no, you've got it all wrong!

AL. You're the one that got it wrong, Mickey – thinkin' you could pull a fast one on Alfonse Feghetti.

(**SHIRLEY** *pulls out Mickey's cigarette case from his breast pocket, opens it, looks inside, shoves it back into Mickey's pocket.*)

SHIRLEY. OK Boss, he's clean.

AL. Stand back, Shirl. I'm gonna grease this weasel.

(**AL** *cocks his gun and aims it at* **MICKEY.**)

MICKEY. *(backing away left)* No Mr. Feghetti, please!

SHIRLEY. Boss, we can't do this here!

MICKEY. You don't need to do it anywhere! I'm innocent, I tell you!

AL. Shut up, Mickey. I heard enough outta you.

(**HONEY** *enters through the archway, carrying a large salmon wrapped in newspaper.*)

MICKEY. Please, Mr. Feghetti! Please! I'm not the guy you want – it was all Bubbalowe's idea! He's the one who stole your booze!

AL. Well we'll be sure to talk to him about that, just before we blow his brains out too! See ya later, Mickey.

(AL shoots, and MICKEY falls to the ground. HONEY screams and runs out. AL AND SHIRLEY turn and see her.)

SHIRLEY. Hey, you! Come back here!

(As they begin to chase after her, FRANK comes running in from the kitchen, sees what's happened, screams, and runs back into the kitchen again. AL AND SHIRLEY turn just in time to see his retreating figure.)

AL. *(pointing the gun at himself)* I'll take her. You take him!

(He exits upstage.)

SHIRLEY. Right, Boss!

(SHIRLEY rushes into the kitchen. As the door swings back, FRANK is discovered clinging to the other side of it. He lets go of the door.)

FRANK. That's it. I don't need a job that badly. *(removing his chef's hat and whites)* Au revoir, Monsieur LaPlouffe.

(HONEY rushes in from the kitchen, minus the salmon, and sees FRANK undressing.)

HONEY. What are you doing?

FRANK. I'm getting out.

HONEY. You can't!

FRANK. Oh yes I can. Do you realize who that was? Alfonse Feghetti!

HONEY. Alfonse Feghetti? THE Alfonse Feghetti? Oh my God!

FRANK. That's right – and when he kills somebody, he doesn't leave any witnesses behind. *(crossing to his suitcase)* I'm leaving. And if you have any smarts, you'll come with me.

HONEY. Wait! You can't leave now!

FRANK. *(picking it up)* I'm sorry to let you down, Miss Bubbalowe, but this is a little more than I bargained for.

(He turns toward the archway.)

HONEY. No, you don't understand. You really *can't* leave. I was just out in the alley – there are gangsters all over the place. We're surrounded!

*(**BUBBALOWE** comes in from the basement.)*

BUBBALOWE. What's going on up here? I thought I heard a shot. *(seeing **MICKEY**)* Oh my God, Mickey! What happened?

HONEY. You've got to hide, Pop! Alfonse Feghetti is here!

BUBBALOWE. Noodles Feghetti is *here*?

HONEY. Yes, he just killed Mickey. And he's going to kill you too!

BUBBALOWE. Me? What for?

HONEY. For stealing his booze!

BUBBALOWE. Oh my God. That little creep Mickey, I'll kill him!

*(He takes to **MICKEY**.)*

FRANK. Too late.

HONEY. You didn't, did you Pop?

BUBBALOWE. What?

HONEY. Steal Feghetti's booze?

BUBBALOWE. Don't be ridiculous! You know me better than that!

HONEY. I'm sorry Pop, I had to ask. Anyway, I've got to get out of here. He's going to kill me too if he finds me.

BUBBALOWE. What?? What's he want to kill you for?

HONEY. I saw them shoot Mickey. And then they saw me. Seeing them.

BUBBALOWE. I see.

HONEY. *(to **BUBBALOWE**)* What did you see?

BUBBALOWE. I didn't see anything! *(turning to **FRANK**)* What did you see?

FRANK. I saw them see her –

(**HONEY** *nudges him, he adopts his French accent.*)

I mean, er, I saw zem see 'er. But zey didn't see me. You see?

BUBBALOWE. I see.

HONEY. And if they see me again, it will be so long.

BUBBALOWE. Sayonara.

FRANK. *(no accent)* See you later. *(heading for the archway, and coming right back in)* Oh no, the gangsters – er, zee gangsters! Here zey come!

BUBBALOWE. *(taking **HONEY**'s hand and racing toward the dining room)* Follow us, Monsieur LaPlouffe!

(**FRANK** *dumps his suitcase near the bar and follows them, a beat behind. As they exit into the dining room, the door swings back and smacks **FRANK** in the face. He falls down. **AL** enters through the archway. **FRANK** crawls under the table as **SHIRLEY** enters from the kitchen.*)

SHIRLEY. Any luck, Boss?

AL. Naw.

SHIRLEY. Me neither.

AL. Well, don't worry. I gave the boys a good description of that dame. If she tries to get away, they'll take care of her.

SHIRLEY. Well, I didn't get a look at the other one, but I did get this. He dropped it on the kitchen floor.

(He holds up a wallet.)

AL. Lemme see that.

(He takes the wallet and looks through it.)

Empty. Figures. Hey, here's his library card. Frank Plunkett. Well at least now we know who we're lookin' for.

(**FRANK** *pokes his head out, gasps, and disappears.*)

SHIRLEY. You see, Boss? This is just the kind of thing I was worried about. Now we got a stiff on our hands and a couple of witnesses runnin' around loose.

AL. They ain't runnin' around loose. They can't go nowhere. The boys are coverin' all the exits.

SHIRLEY. *(pointing to* **MICKEY***)* What do we do with him?

AL. Oh, who cares? Shove him out of sight.

SHIRLEY. *(opening the closet door)* What are we hangin' around for, Boss? Let's lam it out of here before somebody calls the cops!

AL. What, and leave my booze for Morris the Hound?

SHIRLEY. *(stuffing* **MICKEY** *in the closet)* The boys can look after Morris for us.

AL. We ain't goin' nowhere till I've found that Bubbalowe. He's gonna get what's comin' to him. Now come on – let's see if he's hidin' out in the basement.

(They exit into the basement. **FRANK** *scrambles out from under the table.)*

FRANK. Oh my God, what am I gonna do?

(spots the chef's hat, picks it up)

Well Monsieur LaPlouffe, looks like we're stuck with each other for a while!

(He plunks the hat on his head.)

(to the tune of "La Marseillaise") Da da da dum-dum dum-dum DAAA da-dum da da da dum-DUM, da da dum…

(He dashes into the kitchen. **BUBBALOWE** *enters cautiously from the dining room, sees the coast is clear, and races to the phone.)*

BUBBALOWE. *(jiggling the hook)* Operator? Get me the police – and hurry! It's an emergency! *(drumming his fingers on the bar)* Hello, police? You've got to get someone over here right away – there's been a murder!… Château Bubbalowe… Yes, I can tell you who did it – Noodles Feghetti… That's right, THE Noodles Feghetti!… So get someone here fast! If he finds me my goose is cooked... Of course I'm serious! There's a dead man lying right here on my –

(He looks over to where the body was, and sees that it's disappeared.)

Where did he go?... Pardon?... No, this is not a joke! I know a dead body when I see one!

(AL AND SHIRLEY *enter from the basement and see* **BUBBALOWE.***)*

SHIRLEY. Dead body?

BUBBALOWE. Aagh!

AL. Hey, you – who're you talkin' to?

BUBBALOWE. Hm? Who, me?

AL. Yeah.

BUBBALOWE. Oh. *(looking at the phone receiver in his hand)* The uh, undertaker.

SHIRLEY. Undertaker?

BUBBALOWE. *(cringes)* Uh...yes. There's been a death in the family.

(AL AND SHIRLEY *exchange a look.)*

AL. Anybody close?

BUBBALOWE. Oh, no. A very *distant* relative. *(shouting into the wrong end of the phone)* What's that?... Yes, brass handles will be fine. *(into the right end of the phone)* I think that's what she would have wanted. Well, I'll be in touch. Goodbye!

(He hangs up.)

AL. Are you Bubbalowe?

BUBBALOWE. Bubba-who?

SHIRLEY. Bubbalowe. The proprietor.

BUBBALOWE. Never heard of him.

AL. Don't give me that. You got a 50-foot neon sign out there that says Château Bubbalowe on it.

BUBBALOWE. *(suddenly remembering)* Oh! Yes, of course, *that* Mr. Bubbalowe… Well as a matter of fact, he's…you just missed him. He's stepped out.

AL. How long's he gonna be?

BUBBALOWE. Oh, a very, very long time. Perhaps you'd like to come back later.

AL. *(wandering over to the table and seeing the punch)* We'd prefer to wait.

BUBBALOWE. I see.

AL. What's this stuff?

BUBBALOWE. It's punch.

AL. *(to* **SHIRLEY***)* Oh yeah? Probably spiked with my booze.

(He takes a gulp of punch from the ladle and spits it out in horror.)

What the hell's in this?

BUBBALOWE. Oh just some fresh fruit, some juice, a little seltzer. May I tell Mr. Bubbalowe who's calling?

AL. Tell him Alfonse Feghetti wants to see him.

BUBBALOWE. Mr. F-F-F-Feghetti.

(He gulps.)

Pleased to meet you.

(He offers his hand to **AL***, who ignores it.)*

And you are – ?

SHIRLEY. Mr. Feghetti's associate. The name's Shirley.

BUBBALOWE. Shirley? You can't be serious.

SHIRLEY. I am serious. Call me Shirley.

AL. Who are you?

BUBBALOWE. Me? Oh, nobody.

AL. What are you doing here?

BUBBALOWE. I'm uh…I'm the chef. Yeah, that's it. The chef.

SHIRLEY. Oh yeah?

BUBBALOWE. Yeah. I mean, yes. *(backing toward the kitchen)* Listen, I'd love to stay and chat, but I've er – I've got to run – I've gotta finish – plucking my geese.

AL. Get back here. We ain't done with you yet.

>(**BUBBALOWE** *comes back.*)

You don't look like no chef. Where's your hat?

BUBBALOWE. *(improvising madly)* Actually, I haven't had time to change yet. *(seeing* **FRANK***'s suitcase and grabbing it)* I just got off the train.

AL. Oh really? What's your name?

BUBBALOWE. My name? Er – my name is – Plunkett. *(reading from the suitcase)* Frank Plunkett.

AL. Plunkett?!

>(**AL** *and* **SHIRLEY** *pull out their guns.* **SHIRLEY** *grabs* **BUBBALOWE** *by the collar and backs him up against the wall.* **SHIRLEY** *points his gun in* **BUBBALOWE***'s face.*)

BUBBALOWE. Aaagh!! What did I say?

>(*There is the sound of a voice offstage.*)

VOICE. *(off)* Mr. Bubbalowe?

AL. Who the hell is that?

>(**BUBBALOWE** *shrugs.*)

VOICE. *(off)* Hello?

AL. Check it out, Shirl.

>(**SHIRLEY** *crosses to the archway and looks off.*)

You expectin' anyone?

BUBBALOWE. No, no, no one at all.

SHIRLEY. *(rushing over to* **AL***)* Hey, Boss. It's the cops!

AL. The cops? Already?

BUBBALOWE. That was quick.

AL. What was that?

BUBBALOWE. I said, "I feel sick."

AL. You and me both.

>(*We hear the sound of a horse neighing offstage.*)

VOICE. *(off)* Easy, Rosie!

BUBBALOWE. Oh my God, it's Effing.

AL. It's Effing what?

BUBBALOWE. Not Effing what, Effing WHO.

(Another neigh from Rosie, off.)

AL. Well whatever it is, it's effing irritating.

BUBBALOWE. CONSTABLE Effing. He's a Mountie.

SHIRLEY. I told you Boss, we gotta get out of here.

AL. I ain't going nowhere until I seen Bubbalowe.

BUBBALOWE. Oh God.

SHIRLEY. Well then we'd better hide! *(moving toward the dining room)* In here, Boss.

AL. *(still focused on* **BUBBALOWE***)* Okay, okay, I'm comin.' Now you – Plunkett – get rid of him.

BUBBALOWE. Get rid of him?

AL. That's right. And remember, I got twenty of my boys out there. If you try and tip off the cops, they'll be a blood bath out there that'll make the St. Valentine's Day Massacre look like a weenie roast. You got me?

BUBBALOWE. *(gulping)* Got you.

EFFING. *(off)* Mr. Bubbalowe?

BUBBALOWE. *(yelling over his shoulder)* Bubbalowe's not here.

(as **AL AND SHIRLEY** *cross toward the dining room)*

No! Don't go in there –

(They exit into the dining room. **BUBBALOWE** *runs after them. As they exit through one door,* **HONEY** *enters through the other.)*

BUBBALOWE. Honey! Thank God!

HONEY. Pop! They almost saw me.

BUBBALOWE. I know, I know. Quick, in here – *(opening the kitchen door)* and stay out of sight!

(He shoves her into the kitchen, then takes out his hanky and mops his brow. **CONSTABLE HAMILTON X. EFFING** *enters through the archway in full Mountie dress uniform.)*

EFFING. Mr. Bubbalowe?

BUBBALOWE. *(with a look to the dining room)* Ssh, ssh!

EFFING. *(pulling out his gun and looking around, whispering)* What? What is it?

(He turns toward **BUBBALOWE,** *inadvertently pointing his gun at* **BUBBALOWE***'s face.* **BUBBALOWE** *screams and raises his hands.)*

What's wrong? *(looking down at the gun)* Oh. Sorry Mr. Bubbalowe.

BUBBALOWE. SSH!!

EFFING. *(whispering)* What's the matter?

BUBBALOWE. Bad headache. I'm very sensitive to loud noises.

(There is a loud thud from the dining room.)

EFFING. *(turning towards the dining room)* What was that?

BUBBALOWE. *(quickly)* Didn't hear a thing. *(steering him away)* Now, what can I do for you Constable Effing?

EFFING. I'm here about the murder.

(Another thunk. **EFFING** *takes to the dining room door.* **BUBBALOWE** *ignores it.)*

BUBBALOWE. *(incredulous)* Murder?

EFFING. Yes, didn't you just call and report a murder here?

BUBBALOWE. Me? No. I haven't made a phone call all morning.

EFFING. *(taking off his hat and setting it down)* Well somebody called us and reported a murder at Château Bubbalowe. Dispatch took the call not five minutes ago.

BUBBALOWE. Must have been a crank call.

EFFING. I checked with the operator, and she said the call came from here.

BUBBALOWE. She did? Oh, yes – now I remember! I DID make a phone call, but it wasn't to the police. It was to my…uh…supplier. The operator must have got the lines crossed!

EFFING. You called your supplier to report a murder?

BUBBALOWE. No, it had nothing to do with a murder! I was calling about my food order!

EFFING. Food order, eh? *(referring to his notes)* Then why did you tell the dispatcher that there was a dead man in the room?

BUBBALOWE. Dead man in the room? No, no! I didn't say there WAS a dead man, I'd said I'd BE a dead man if I didn't get my order! You see, I've got sixty guests coming for my grand opening tonight!

EFFING. Uh-huh. Then what did you mean when you said your goose was cooked?

BUBBALOWE. My goose IS cooked. I mean, it will be. That's the entrée – Goose Gallantine!

EFFING. *(still reading)* And what about this reference to Noodles Feghetti?

BUBBALOWE. *(his mind racing)* Noodles Feghetti? I didn't say "Feghetti," I said "spaghetti." That's one of the side dishes!

EFFING. Goose with spaghetti on the side?

BUBBALOWE. Oh yes. It's very popular. They're serving it in all the best restaurants these days.

(He turns away and mops his brow.)

Now I'm very sorry for all the confusion, Constable Effing, but as I'm sure you can understand, I've got a lot on my plate at the moment – ha ha ha! *(crossing to the closet door)* So if you don't mind, I really must get back to laying my tables.

EFFING. *(starts to go for his hat)* Alright, Mr. Bubbalowe. I'll go back and check it out with Dispatch. I must say the whole thing did sound a bit odd.

BUBBALOWE. Anyway, if there were a murder, there would be a body here, right? And as you can see, Constable, there's no body here but me. Ha ha –

*(He opens the closet door and **MICKEY**'s upright body begins to tumble out.)*

(screaming) Haaaaah!!!!!

(He slams the door closed. **EFFING** *turns to him.)*

EFFING. What was that?

BUBBALOWE. What was what? Oh, that was....our chef.

EFFING. What's he screaming about?

BUBBALOWE. No, he's not screaming, he's warming up his voice!

EFFING. I beg your pardon?

BUBBALOWE. He's François LaPlouffe, the singing chef!

EFFING. You mean you have THE François LaPlouffe working in your kitchen?

BUBBALOWE. That's right! And we're very lucky to have him.

EFFING. Oh, my wife is a huge fan of his. Do you think he'd be good enough to give me an autograph? She'd be thrilled!

BUBBALOWE. Well, he's a little busy at the moment, but perhaps you'd like to join us tonight. You can see him perform!

EFFING. I'm afraid I have other plans this evening. You see, I'm getting promoted to corporal today.

BUBBALOWE. Really? So that's why you're in your dress uniform.

EFFING. Yes, and that's why I'm riding Rosie today.

BUBBALOWE. I beg your pardon?

EFFING. Rosie, my horse. She's getting promoted as well.

BUBBALOWE. *(offering his hand)* Really. Well, congratulations to you both!

EFFING. Thank you.

BUBBALOWE. *(ushering him toward the archway)* Perhaps you and your wife can join us some other night, then. I'm sure Monsieur LaPlouffe would be happy to meet you.

EFFING. That's very kind of you, Mr. Bubbalowe. I'll definitely take you up on that.

(He exits. **BUBBALOWE** *mops his brow.* **AL** *and* **SHIRLEY** *peek out into the room.)*

AL. Psst! Plunkett. All clear?

BUBBALOWE. All clear.

(**AL** *and* **SHIRLEY** *emerge from the dining room.*)

AL. Good. *(as they point their guns in* **BUBBALOWE***'s face)* Now where were we?

BUBBALOWE. Wait a minute! Wait a minute! What do you want to kill me for?

AL. It's nothin' personal, Plunkett, but I can't afford to leave no witnesses behind.

BUBBALOWE. Are you talking about Mickey? Hey, I didn't see a thing. And anyway, as far as I'm concerned, he got what was coming to him. He was a crook! No offence.

SHIRLEY. None taken.

AL. Sorry, Plunkett, but business is business.

(He cocks his gun.)

BUBBALOWE. WAIT!! Please don't kill me! You need me!

AL. Oh yeah? What do I need you for?

BUBBALOWE. Well for one thing, to protect you from Effing.

AL. From effing what?

BUBBALOWE. Not Effing what, Effing who – the Mountie! I mean, I got rid of him once, didn't I?

AL. So?

BUBBALOWE. What are you going to do if he comes back? Look, you need someone who's familiar with the territory, who knows how things work around here. I can help you.

SHIRLEY. You know Boss, he's got a point.

BUBBALOWE. I sure do!

SHIRLEY. He can help keep the cops off our back till we get the merchandise out of here.

BUBBALOWE. I sure can!

SHIRLEY. And he can also lead us to Bubbalowe.

BUBBALOWE. I sure will – Bubbalowe??!

AL. Yeah. He's the one that cooked up this heist with Mickey.

BUBBALOWE. Mr. Bubbalowe? Oh no, Mr. Feghetti, he didn't have anything to do with it. It was all Mickey's idea. He tricked Mr. Bubbalowe into storing the stuff here. He said it was just pea soup.

AL. Oh, I see. And Bubbalowe swallowed this story, did he?

BUBBALOWE. *(tearfully)* Yes, yes, he did. *(confidentially)* You know, between you and me, Mr. Bubbalowe's a real nice guy – but he's not very bright.

AL. Look, Plunkett, nobody's that stupid. If that creep Mickey shipped five hundred cases of my booze into this joint then Bubbalowe had to know about it. *(to* **SHIRLEY**) Amateurs. Can you believe this Bubbalowe, thinking he could pull off a stunt like this? Doesn't he realize what I'm going to have to do to him?

BUBBALOWE. *(gulping)* Do to him?

AL. Oh yeah. We got big plans for him.

BUBBALOWE. Plans? What kind of plans?

AL. Oh, you know. Dis and dat.

SHIRLEY. Dislocation, dismemberment, disembowelment…

BUBBALOWE. *(bleating with fear)* Ah-ah-ah-ah-ah.

SHIRLEY. You okay, Plunkett? You don't look so good.

BUBBALOWE. *(holding his stomach)* Just a little – dyspeptic.

AL. Huh?

BUBBALOWE. Look, Mr. Feghetti, take my word for it – Mr. Bubbalowe had no idea this was your property. If I'd known – I mean, I know Mr. Bubbalowe – as well as I know myself. He'd never go along with something like this – he's dead against bootlegging!

AL. Oh he's dead alright.

BUBBALOWE. Believe me, he would never steal anything from anybody. He's a good egg.

AL. By the time I'm done with him he'll be a scrambled egg.

EFFING. *(off)* Excuse me again!

BUBBALOWE. It's Effing. He's back!

AL. Get rid of him, Plunkett – *(puts the gun in* **BUBBALOWE***'s face)* and make sure he doesn't find my booze.

SHIRLEY. Quick, Boss!

*(***AL** *and* **SHIRLEY** *race into the dining room just as* **EFFING** *enters through the archway.)*

EFFING. I hate to trouble you again, Mr. Bubbalowe –

BUBBALOWE. *(holding his head)* SSHH!!

EFFING. *(whispering)* Sorry. I forgot my hat.

*(***EFFING** *crosses to the table downstage right to get his hat. He sees the punch.)*

Hmm. What's this?

BUBBALOWE. What's what? Oh that? It's punch. It's for my guests.

EFFING. *(joking)* Not spiked is it?

BUBBALOWE. *(laughing a little too loudly)* No, of course not.

EFFING. Looks rather tasty. Do you mind if I have some?

BUBBALOWE. Go right ahead.

*(***EFFING** *sets his hat back down, picks up a glass and starts helping himself.)*

EFFING. Mmm, this is delicious. You know I've never understood why someone would want to spoil a perfectly good drink like this by filling it full of alcohol.

BUBBALOWE. *(crossing to the table)* You're not a drinking man, I take it.

EFFING. I never touch the stuff. I've always been a big campaigner against the evils of drink. It brings nothing but trouble. Attracts the criminal element.

BUBBALOWE. *(with a look to the dining room)* You're telling me.

EFFING. Look at what's happened to this town lately. You may not be aware of this, but gangsters like Alfonse Feghetti have been using Niagara Falls as a liquor pipeline for years. That's why I was so interested when the dispatcher told me you'd mentioned his name.

BUBBALOWE. *(innocently)* Alfonse Feghetti the Chicago gangster?

EFFING. That's right. He operates out of a place here in town. Maybe you've heard of it – Dominion Warehouse.

BUBBALOWE. *(with a take to the few remaining boxes)* Dominion Warehouse?

EFFING. Yes, we've had our eye on it for quite a while now. Haven't been able to shut them down yet, but it's only a matter of time.

BUBBALOWE. Gosh, I didn't realize...

EFFING. Yes, it's a very serious problem in this town. In fact, it's been my sad duty to shut down many establishments just like this one because of their involvement in the rum-running trade.

BUBBALOWE. *(leaning on the bar)* Well Constable, you're not going to have to worry about shutting me down. I've invested far too much in this place to risk it all by getting involved in bootlegging. Now if there's nothing else –

(As **EFFING** *picks up his hat,* **BUBBALOWE** *see the bottle of whiskey that Al and Shirley left on the bar. He screams and picks it up, trying to figure out how to conceal it.* **EFFING** *turns.)*

EFFING. What was that?

BUBBALOWE. Hm?

(He shoves the bottle down the front of his pants with the cork pointing down and turns to **EFFING.***)*

What was what?

EFFING. You screamed.

BUBBALOWE. Ah yes, so I did. Ahh!! *(bending over and holding his back)* Sorry. Kidney stone. It flares up every once in a while.

(There is a loud pop as the cork comes out of the bottle in **BUBBALOWE***'s pants, followed by the sound of the bottle disgorging itself. The realization of what's happening dawns on* **BUBBALOWE***'s face.* **EFFING** *and*

BUBBALOWE's *focus is drawn first to the stain in* **BUBBALOWE**'s *pants and down his leg to the growing puddle on the floor.)*

BUBBALOWE. I think it just passed.

(a beat)

I'm very sorry. Excuse me just a moment.

*(**BUBBALOWE** scurries behind the bar. **EFFING**, eyes glued to the puddle, steps away and slowly lifts up one foot and examines the sole of his shoe. Taking advantage of **EFFING**'s distraction, **BUBBALOWE** removes the bottle from his pants and quickly tosses it down the chute. He then bends down to find a rag from under the bar. A crash is heard as the bottle hits the basement floor.)*

EFFING. *(looking towards the bar)* What was that?

BUBBALOWE. *(appearing from behind the bar, rag in hand)* Sorry?

EFFING. That loud crash.

BUBBALOWE. I didn't hear anything.

(He crosses to the puddle and starts to clean up the mess.)

EFFING. Look, I'm beginning to think – what's that smell?

BUBBALOWE. What smell?

EFFING. *(sniffing the air)* Smells like – liquor.

BUBBALOWE. *(desperately cleaning up the puddle)* I don't smell a thing.

(He smells the rag and almost gags.)

EFFING. *(picking up the glass he was drinking from and sniffing at it)* You sure there isn't any alcohol in this punch?

BUBBALOWE. *(finishes cleaning up and crosses to the bar with the rag)* No, of course not.

EFFING. Well, it's coming from somewhere.

(He puts his nose into the bowl of punch and **BUBBALOWE** *takes the opportunity to sling the rag down the chute. He slams it shut and immediately stands in front of it trying to look innocent.)*

EFFING. What's going on here?

BUBBALOWE. Going on?

EFFING. You're behaving very strangely.

BUBBALOWE. Am I?

EFFING. Look, Mr. Bubbalowe –

BUBBALOWE. *(with a panicked look to the dining room)* SSSSSHHHH!

(He grabs his head and mimes much pain.)

EFFING. *(impatiently)* I'm not a fool. You're obviously up to something. And I'm going to find out what it is.

BUBBALOWE. Please, Constable Effing, you must excuse my behaviour; it's just that I'm under a lot of pressure right now. I assure you I'm not up to anything.

EFFING. Good. Then you won't mind if I sniff around a bit then.

(He heads towards the boxes of pea soup. BUBBALOWE *follows him.)*

(spying the boxes) What's in here?

BUBBALOWE. *(ducking in front of* EFFING*)* Nothing important. Just – supplies.

(He puts his foot up on one of them and leans on his knee.)

EFFING. Oh really? Let's have a look. *(reading the side of the box)* I see they're from Dominion Warehouse.

BUBBALOWE. *(feigning amazement)* Are they? *(looks at the box and then immediately leans on it again)* My, my, so they are.

EFFING. *(dubiously)* French Canadian pea soup, eh?

BUBBALOWE. That's right.

EFFING. All of this?

BUBBALOWE. Yes, we decided to stock up on it. We get a good deal when we buy it by the gross.

EFFING. That's an awful lot of pea soup. What are you going to do with it?

BUBBALOWE. Oh, this stuff's going to put us on the culinary map! It's quite a delicacy in Quebec, you know. They eat it cold. I've even invented my own name for it – Pea-chyssoise.

EFFING. Very catchy. Let's have a look, shall we?

(He motions for **BUBBALOWE** *to move out of the way. The phone rings.* **EFFING** *looks toward the phone.* **BUBBALOWE** *sits down on one box and stretches his legs out across the other one. He immediately becomes fascinated with his fingernails.* **EFFING** *looks back to* **BUBBALOWE** *and registers his surprise.)*

EFFING. Now what are you up to?

BUBBALOWE. Hmm? Oh, just taking the weight off my feet.

EFFING. Aren't you going to answer that?

BUBBALOWE. Answer what?

EFFING. *(losing patience)* The phone! It's ringing!

BUBBALOWE. *(not moving)* Is it? Oh well, never mind. Probably nothing important.

(The phone rings again.)

EFFING. *(crossing to phone)* Heck of a way to run a business.

(He picks up the phone.)

(answers) Hello… Yes, this is Château Bubbalowe… *(surprised)* This is Constable Effing speaking… *(snapping to attention)* Yes, Superintendent… What?… I see… The Dominion Warehouse, eh?…

*(***EFFING** *takes to* **BUBBALOWE** *who affects an even more nonchalant attitude.)*

Thank you… Yes Sir, I'll be right there.

(He hangs up.)

BUBBALOWE. *(fishing)* Sounds serious.

EFFING. Arson generally is.

BUBBALOWE. Arson??!

EFFING. *(putting on his hat)* Yes, someone's put a torch to Dominion Warehouse. It's got all the earmarks of a gangland hit, apparently. I've got to get over there and investigate.

BUBBALOWE. *(leaping up and ushering* **EFFING** *out toward the archway)* Well, good luck, Constable.

EFFING. Don't think you're off the hook yet, Bubbalowe.

*(***BUBBALOWE*** *looks to the dining room and winces.)*

I'll be back. I know you're mixed up with this somehow.

(He exits through the archway.)

BUBBALOWE. *(mopping his face with his hanky)* Dear God.

(He looks down, cringes at his wet pants and proceeds to take them off. He races to the chute and throws them down as **AL AND SHIRLEY** *peek in from the dining room.)*

AL. Hey Plunkett.

BUBBALOWE. Aagh!

(He turns around.)

AL. What are you doin' in your skivvies?

BUBBALOWE. Never mind!

(He grabs his tuxedo pants and puts them on during the following.)

SHIRLEY. So what happened to the Mountie?

BUBBALOWE. He had to go and investigate a fire at Dominion Warehouse.

*(***AL AND SHIRLEY*** *look to one another.)*

AL. The boys didn't waste any time, did they?

BUBBALOWE. No, and neither will Effing. He knows something's up, and he'll be back. You'd better get this booze out of here while you've got the chance.

*(***FRANK*** *enters from the kitchen.)*

FRANK. Monsieur Bubbaloo –

(seeing the gangsters)

AGH! Excusez-moi –

(He turns to go back to the kitchen.)

BUBBALOWE. What is it, Monsieur LaPlouffe?

*(**FRANK** stops, turns around again, terrified.)*

AL. So you're LaPoof are you? The famous singin' chef?

FRANK. *(no accent)* Singing chef?

BUBBALOWE. That's right.

AL. No kiddin'! Hey, I always wanted to meet you. Why don't you do somethin' for us? How about some Pagliacci?

FRANK. *(French accent)* Pagliacci? Oh, I'm all out at zee moment. How about a little linguine instead?

AL. Huh? Oh, I get it. *(chuckling)* Hey, you're pretty funny, LaPoof. No, come on – do a song for us. You know, some opera.

FRANK. *(no accent)* OPERA?? *(accent again)* Oh no, zat is – *(French pronunciation)* impossible. I uh, I never sing in zee daytime. Eet ees very bad luck.

AL. Really?

SHIRLEY. Boss, I think we oughta get movin'.

BUBBALOWE. Yes, Mr. Feghetti. We don't have much time.

AL. Yeah, yeah. Well, it was nice to meet you, LaPoof. Boy, wait'll I tell my mother about this. She'll never believe it!

*(**FRANK** dashes into the kitchen.)*

SHIRLEY. I'll go get a couple of the boys to give us a hand.

AL. OK – and tell 'em to back that truck up to the kitchen door.

SHIRLEY. Right, Boss.

(He exits through the archway.)

AL. Come on Plunkett, let's get those boxes outta here. You can start with these.

*(He indicates the remaining two boxes on the set. **BUBBALOWE** picks them up as **SHIRLEY** rushes back in.)*

SHIRLEY. Hey Boss! That lady cop's back!

BUBBALOWE. Lady cop?

AL. *(straightening his tie)* Really?

SHIRLEY. *(grabbing his arm)* Boss – this ain't the time! Come on, we better get outta sight.

BUBBALOWE. *(opening the closet door)* Quick. In here. And here, take these!

(He hands the last of the boxes to **SHIRLEY** *as* **AL** *and* **SHIRLEY** *exit into the closet.* **VERONICA** *enters through the archway.)*

VERONICA. Mr. Bubbalowe?

BUBBALOWE. Yes? *(with a look to the closet door, whispering)* I mean, yes, that's me. But please – call me Frank.

VERONICA. *(a little thrown, whispering in response)* Alright, uh, Frank. I'm Veronica Snook. *(handing him a card)* I was here earlier.

BUBBALOWE. *(reading, regular voice)* "Government of Cana-da"? What department?

VERONICA. I'm with the Immigration Branch.

BUBBALOWE. Immigration?

VERONICA. Yes. I'm looking for one of your employees. François LaPlouffe.

BUBBALOWE. Why? Is there a problem?

VERONICA. Yes, Frank, there is. He's on the run, you see. I planned to arrest him this morning on the train from Toronto, but he gave me the slip before I could find him.

BUBBALOWE. On the run? Why?

VERONICA. He's a Communist, Frank.

BUBBALOWE. Communist?

VERONICA. I'm afraid so. He tried to get the kitchen staff at the Royal York Hotel to form a union!

BUBBALOWE. *(appalled)* A union? How horrible!

VERONICA. Our sentiments exactly.

BUBBALOWE. *(with a look to the kitchen)* I hope he doesn't think he's going to start any of that nonsense here.

VERONICA. Well, I'm here to make sure he doesn't.

BUBBALOWE. I can't believe it! I was wondering how Honey managed to hire him away from the Royal York.

VERONICA. Well now you know. And that's why we're deporting him.

BUBBALOWE. What??

VERONICA. That's what we usually do with subversives. *(clocking his reaction)* You certainly don't expect us to let people like that go running around free, do you?

BUBBALOWE. *(caught out)* Hmm? No, of course not.

VERONICA. I was hoping you'd feel that way. Now, if you don't mind I'd like to speak with him.

BUBBALOWE. *(with a look to the kitchen)* Oh, er, I'm sorry to tell you this, Miss Snook, but Mr. LaPlouffe's not here. We were expecting him on that train this morning, but he wasn't on it.

VERONICA. Is that so? Well, perhaps I'll go down to the station and see what they know there. He may have booked a ticket on the next train. I'll check back with you later.

BUBBALOWE. Alright, Miss Snook.

(She exits. **FRANK** *enters from the kitchen.)*

FRANK. Monsieur Bubbaloo –

BUBBALOWE. Monsieur LaPlouffe! Why didn't you tell me Immigration was after you?

FRANK. *(no accent)* Huh?

BUBBALOWE. I just had some woman here from the Immigration Branch who wants to run you out of the country.

FRANK. WHAT??

BUBBALOWE. Forming a union indeed!

FRANK. Union?

BUBBALOWE. And don't get any ideas about starting any Communist uprisings here! I won't stand for it.

FRANK. No, sir. I mean non, Monsieur.

BUBBALOWE. Anyway, I've gotten rid of her – for the time being, at least. But from now on, if anyone asks, you are not a chef, and you're not François LaPlouffe. Do you understand?

FRANK. Um…

BUBBALOWE. Good. Now, take your clothes off.

FRANK. *(no accent)* I beg your pardon?

> *(**BUBBALOWE** tears off **FRANK**'s chef's coat and hat. He still wears his shirt and dark pants.)*

BUBBALOWE. You've got to get out of those whites! If Veronica Snook sees you dressed like a chef and talking with that accent, she's going to know who you are. And quite frankly, Maestro, commie or not, I can't afford to lose you right now! So here, put this on –

> *(He hands **FRANK** his tuxedo jacket. It's not even close to the right size.)*

FRANK. But Monsieur Bubbaloo –

BUBBALOWE. *(with a take to the closet door)* And don't call me Bubbaloo – er Bubbalowe! As far as you're concerned, Irving Bubbalowe is dead. From now on my name is Plunkett. Comprenday? Frank Plunkett!!

FRANK. *(no accent)* Frank Plunkett?!!!

> *(**EFFING** enters through the archway and crosses straight to **BUBBALOWE**.)*

EFFING. Aha! Bubbalowe!

FRANK. No – zee name's "Frank."

BUBBALOWE. *(to **FRANK**)* Ssh!

EFFING. *(to **BUBBALOWE**)* Now listen, Bubbalowe –

FRANK. 'E's not Bubbalowe I tell you!

BUBBALOWE. Shut up!

EFFING. I beg your pardon?

BUBBALOWE. Not you, Constable.

EFFING. Frankly, Bubbalowe I've had –

FRANK. *(insistently)* It is not Frankie Bubbalowe, eet is Frankie Plunkett.

EFFING. What? Who is this "Frank" you keep babbling about?

FRANK AND BUBBALOWE. *(pointing to each other)* Him.

EFFING. Huh?

BUBBALOWE. You must excuse him, Constable, he's just trying to introduce himself to you. This is Frank – er – Frank Pagliacci –

FRANK. Pagliacci?

EFFING. Pagliacci eh? That's Italian isn't it?

FRANK. Oui. Er, si.

   (meekly) Buon giorno.

EFFING. How do you do? Now, Bubbalowe –

FRANK. *(Italian accent)* No, no you 'ave it-a wrong! 'Ees not Bubbalowe – Bubbalowe eesa dead!

EFFING. Dead?

BUBBALOWE. No no! Nobody's dead. *(grabbing FRANK)* Er, thank you "Frank." Don't mind him, Constable, he's a little confused.

FRANK. You can a-say that again.

BUBBALOWE. Now what can I do for you?

EFFING. You can start by explaining what that hearse is doing here.

BUBBALOWE. Hearse?

EFFING. Yes, there's a hearse parked in the alley.

BUBBALOWE. Oh. Yes. So there is. *(indicating FRANK)* It's his hearse.

FRANK. It is?

   (BUBBALOWE nudges him.)

   Oh. Yes. Eet is.

BUBBALOWE. He's the undertaker.

FRANK. Undertaker?!!

EFFING. Ah-ha! So there is a body here after all.

FRANK. Mama Mia!

EFFING. What was that?

FRANK. I just-a said Mama Mia –

BUBBALOWE. Yes, yes! That's it! Mama Mia!

EFFING. Huh?

BUBBALOWE. Mr. Pagliacci's here for my mama. Mia Bubba-lowe!

FRANK. What? *(off BUBBALOWE's glare, Italian accent)* Oh. Si. It's a-true. Mama Bubbalowe has-a passed on.

(BUBBALOWE bursts into tears, pulls out his hanky and blows his nose noisily.)

EFFING. *(taking off his hat)* Oh. I'm sorry. I didn't realize. What happened?

FRANK. *(Italian accent)* It was a-quite unexpected. One-a minute she was peelin' the potatoes and the next –

(He makes a loud raspberry sound.)

Face first into the salmon-a mousse.

EFFING. How tragic.

(HONEY enters from the kitchen, carrying the salmon on a large dish.)

HONEY. Oh, Monsieur LaPlouffe, I was wondering –

EFFING. LaPlouffe?

(FRANK looks to BUBBALOWE.)

BUBBALOWE. Er, no, Monsieur LaPlouffe's stepped out for a moment. This is Signor Pagliacci!

HONEY. Pagliacci?

FRANK. Si. Frank Pagliacci of Pagliacci, Puccini and – Papadopoulos. Undertakers at large. *(pulling his business card out of his pocket)* My card.

(He holds it out to HONEY, who reaches for it. FRANK immediately puts it in his pocket. HONEY looks completely flummoxed.)

BUBBALOWE. This is my daughter Honey, Constable.

EFFING. *(offering his hand)* How do you do, Miss Bubbalowe. Hamilton Xavier Effing. I'm sorry to meet you under such sad circumstances. This must have come as quite a shock to you.

HONEY. Shock?

*(Behind **EFFING**'s back, **FRANK** is madly signalling for **HONEY** to play along. She looks confused. **EFFING** turns to see **FRANK** waving his hands about. **FRANK** kills an imaginary fly with his hands, and wipes them on his pants.)*

EFFING. *(turning back to **HONEY**)* Er, yes. Your grandmother.

HONEY. Grandmother?

EFFING. Yes, her passing away so unexpectedly.

HONEY. But grandmother's been dead for fifteen –

FRANK. *(cutting her off)* MINUTES!!

(beat)

Sorry.

BUBBALOWE. Yes, it was very sudden.

EFFING. *(to **FRANK**)* Fifteen minutes? You didn't waste any time getting here, did you, Mr. Pagliacci?

FRANK. Well-a business 'as a-been a leetle slow.

EFFING. *(sniffing, to **FRANK**)* What's that smell?

*(**FRANK** checks under his arms.)*

HONEY. Oh, I'm sorry. That must be the salmon.

EFFING. Salmon?

BUBBALOWE. Yes. Needless to say, after mother's demise we had to replace the mousse.

EFFING. Alright, I've heard enough. What's going on here?

BUBBALOWE. Going on? Nothing.

EFFING. What kind of an idiot do you take me for? It's obvious you're covering something up.

HONEY. What do you mean, Constable?

EFFING. Well I'm sorry to tell you this, Miss Bubbalowe, but I have reason to believe your father's been involved in a murder.

HONEY. Murder?

EFFING. An employee at the Dominion Warehouse. Mickey McCall.

BUBBALOWE. That's ridiculous.

EFFING. Is it? Then perhaps you can explain why you called to report that Noodles Feghetti had murdered somebody here?

BUBBALOWE. Uh –

EFFING. And why Dominion Warehouse (an operation with direct connections to Noodles Feghetti) has just been burned to the ground – on top of which, Mickey McCall, the manager of the Warehouse and known associate of Feghetti's, has mysteriously disappeared after making a delivery here. A delivery which, I have on good authority, consists of 500 cases of Noodles Feghetti's liquor.

HONEY. What?

EFFING. That's right, Miss; and now, I find a hearse parked out in the alley surrounded by a bunch of shady-looking characters in striped suits and fedoras. It's obvious what's happened here.

BUBBALOWE AND HONEY. It is?

EFFING. Of course. You and Mickey had some kind of deal going with Feghetti. The deal went sour, Mickey was killed, and now you're covering it up. Right?

BUBBALOWE. Wrong. Listen, Constable Effing, you have to believe me; I had nothing to do with any of this. I mean, what would a guy like me be doing mixed up with someone like Noodles Feghetti?

EFFING. Bootlegging.

BUBBALOWE. Bootlegging? I told you before, I'd never get involved with something like that.

EFFING. Oh really? Then what about those five hundred cases of liquor that were delivered here?

BUBBALOWE. I don't know what you're talking about.

EFFING. Well, if that's true, you won't mind if I take a look around, will you?

(He heads for the basement.)

HONEY. Constable Effing, there's no need for any of this. We're just trying to open a restaurant here, that's all. Believe me, my father would never be mixed up with gangsters. He's the most honest person I know.

EFFING. There's something very fishy going on here, and I'm not talking about the salmon.

BUBBALOWE. Salmon? Oh my God, the mousse! *(checking his watch)* We'll never be ready at this rate. Honey, you'd better get back in the kitchen – and take Signor Pagliacci with you!

HONEY. Come on – er – Signor. We have to work to do.

FRANK. Ah, si! I 'ave to start gutting the goose.

EFFING. *(horrified, thinking he means "grandmother")* I beg your pardon?

FRANK. *(realizing what he's just said)* So to speak.

EFFING. Wait a minute, Mr. Pagliacci – why are you going into the kitchen?

FRANK. *(freezing in his tracks)* Um. *(turning to* **EFFING***)* That's where Mama Bubbalowe is.

EFFING. You've got a body in the kitchen?

FRANK. Hey, don't-a worry – we put her in-a the icebox.

*(***HONEY*** reacts. ***FRANK*** grabs her by the hand and hauls her into the kitchen.)*

EFFING. A body in the kitchen, eh? I think I'd better take a look in there myself.

*(He turns toward the kitchen. ***BUBBALOWE****, panicked, runs in front of him in an attempt to intercept him just as we hear a scuffling noise from the closet. ***EFFING*** and ***BUBBALOWE*** freeze, and take to the closet door.)*

What was that?

BUBBALOWE. *(hopefully)* Rats?

EFFING. Rats in the closet and a dead body in the icebox? I think I'd better call in the Health Department.

(There is a loud thump from the closet.)

EFFING. *(suspicious)* Those sound like pretty big rats.

BUBBALOWE. Yes, it's a real problem in this neighbourhood.

(We hear AL and SHIRLEY grunting and groaning in the closet.)

EFFING. OK, that's it.

(He marches over to the closet and opens the door. SHIRLEY, AL and MICKEY are discovered in a row, dressed as chefs. MICKEY is between AL and SHIRLEY, his arms draped around AL. SHIRLEY is behind MICKEY with his hand down the back of MICKEY's pants. AL has his cigar in his mouth. BUBBALOWE is terrified.)

EFFING. What the – what are you doing?

SHIRLEY. I uh, lost my keys. I was just looking for them.

EFFING. In *his* pants? Alright you three, come out of the closet.

(AL and SHIRLEY come out, supporting MICKEY between them. They leave the door open behind them and cross to center.)

Looks like you've got some Nancy-boys working for you here.

AL. *(infuriated)* Who you callin' a Nancy-boy, Clown?

(SHIRLEY attempts to restrain AL as BUBBALOWE steps in to defuse matters.)

BUBBALOWE. Uh, Constable Effing, this is my kitchen staff. *(indicating SHIRLEY)* This is er… Mr. Humphrey, my pastry chef.

SHIRLEY. Charmed, I'm sure.

BUBBALOWE. *(indicating AL)* And this is Mr. uh, Dumphries. The bus-boy.

AL. *(outraged)* Bus-boy?

BUBBALOWE. *(taking the cigar out of AL's mouth)* Now Dumphries, you know there's no smoking on the job.

(He slaps AL's hand. AL glares at him.)

EFFING. *(indicating* **MICKEY***)* And who is this?

BUBBALOWE. Er – this is – this is – the Maestro himself – François LaPlouffe!

EFFING. François LaPlouffe!

(impressed, grabbing **MICKEY***'s hand and pumping it, assisted by* **AL***)*

Well it's an honour to meet you, Monsieur.

(letting go of the hand, which flops back down, to **BUB-BALOWE***)*

He doesn't look too well.

BUBBALOWE. No, he's – er – been overdoing it a little lately. You know how it is? Working too hard.

EFFING. Oh, yes, I know all about that.

SHIRLEY. Yeh, he's really dead on his feet.

*(***AL*** whacks* **SHIRLEY** *from behind.* **BUBBALOWE** *surreptitiously creeps up to the basement door, and begins fumbling with his keys.)*

EFFING. What were you all doing in the closet?

AL. Truth is, Officer, Mr. LaPoof's got a bit of a drinkin' problem.

EFFING. *(astounded)* No.

AL. 'Fraid so. *(conspiratorially)* He's been dippin' into the sauce. And I'm not talkin' about no Heinz 57. We was just tryin' to sober him up.

EFFING. In the closet?

SHIRLEY. The boss don't like him to be seen like this. It ain't good for business.

EFFING. No, I'm sure it ain't. Isn't.

AL. Maybe we should let him lie down and sleep it off.

SHIRLEY. Good idea, Boss. I mean, er, Dumpty. *(to* **EFFING***)* 'Scuze us.

*(***AL AND SHIRLEY*** walk* **MICKEY** *over to the table and sit him down.* **SHIRLEY** *arranges him so that his head is on his hands on the table.)*

EFFING. *(crossing to* **BUBBALOWE***)* Drinking on the job eh? And how would he get his hands on the stuff, I wonder?

BUBBALOWE. *(shoving the keys back in his pocket)* I'm sure he simply bought it himself. Alcohol is legal in this country, after all.

EFFING. Not in a public house, it isn't. I think I'll just see what else you're hiding in that closet.

BUBBALOWE. But Constable –

*(***EFFING*** spots the pea soup boxes.)*

EFFING. Aha! What have we here?

*(***EFFING*** picks up a couple of boxes and brings them out.)*

Some more of your famous pea soup?

*(***BUBBALOWE*** gasps.)*

Something wrong?

BUBBALOWE. *(in a strangled voice)* Another kidney stone.

(He doubles over again.)

EFFING. You don't mind if I have a look in here do you?

BUBBALOWE. Habedahabedahabeda.

SHIRLEY. Sure. Go right ahead.

BUBBALOWE. *(looking at* **SHIRLEY** *with surprise)* Huh?

*(***EFFING*** opens it with great relish, as* **BUBBALOWE** *whimpers.* **EFFING** *pulls out a couple of cans.)*

EFFING. What the heck?

(He reaches in and pulls out a couple more cans.)

What's this? Pork and beans?

*(***BUBBALOWE*** practically faints in relief.* **AL** *and* **SHIRLEY** *are smiling triumphantly and nudging one another.)*

AL. What's the matter, Officer? You got somethin' against pork and beans?

SHIRLEY. *(to* **BUBBALOWE***)* Uh, Boss, shouldn't me and Mr. Dumpty here be gettin' back to work?

BUBBALOWE. Oh, yes. Good idea.

SHIRLEY. *(gleefully)* Come on, Dumpty. You ain't finished moppin' that floor in the kitchen.

EFFING. Just a minute. Nobody's going anywhere until I've searched this place – starting with the basement. Now, let's go.

(He starts towards the basement door. **BUBBALOWE** *races in front of him and surreptitiously locks the door.)*

BUBBALOWE. I'm telling you, Constable. You're wasting your time!

*(***AL*** *pulls a gun out and aims it at the back of* **EFFING** *'s head.* **SHIRLEY** *tries to wrestle it away from him.* **EFFING** *turns to see what the commotion is about, and discovers* **SHIRLEY** *with his arms draped around* **AL***. They both smile at him, as innocently as they can.)*

EFFING. What is it with you two? Can't you keep your hands off each other for five minutes?

*(***AL*** *shrugs* **SHIRLEY** *off.)*

BUBBALOWE. He can't help himself. He's very possessive.

EFFING. I really don't want to know about their personal lives. *(crossing to the basement door)* Now let's get downstairs, I haven't got all day.

*(***AL*** *pulls a bottle out from under his chef's hat and prepares to cosh* **EFFING** *over the head with it.* **EFFING** *tries the door, finds it's locked, then turns around.)*

It's locked.

(As **EFFING** *turns,* **AL** *hides the bottle behind his back.* **SHIRLEY** *grabs it from him and* **AL** *is left in a provocative pose facing* **EFFING***. He smiles.* **EFFING** *steps back, thinking* **AL** *is coming on to him.)*

What have you done with the key, Bubbalowe?

AL. Bubbalowe?

*(***AL*** *and* **SHIRLEY** *turn to look for* **BUBBALOWE** *behind them. Seeing this,* **BUBBALOWE** *follows suit.)*

Who's he talking to?

BUBBALOWE. *(shrugging)* Don't ask me.

(There is a loud explosion from the kitchen. They all jump and turn toward the kitchen. **AL** *and* **SHIRLEY** *back up, pulling out their guns.)*

EFFING. What was that?

AL. *(overlapping)* What's going on?

BUBBALOWE. *(overlapping)* My God! What now?

*(***HONEY*** comes running in from the kitchen, dressed in whites, with a chef's hat on and carrying dishcloth. Her face is black with soot. Smoke pours out of the kitchen.)*

HONEY. He-e-elp!

(She sees **AL** *and* **SHIRLEY,** *their guns drawn, and lets out another scream.* **EFFING** *turns to see what* **HONEY** *was screaming at, but* **AL** *and* **SHIRLEY** *have put away their guns. They smile at him, benignly.)*

BUBBALOWE. What's happened?

*(***HONEY,*** terrified, attempts to speak, but can manage only a few inarticulate, guttural sounds.)*

HONEY. He – hmm – ah – wwwaaaahhh!!!

EFFING. Who are you?

HONEY. *(wailing)* Aiieee! OOohhh!! Waaannnhhh!!!

EFFING. What was that?

BUBBALOWE. Oh, you'll have to excuse my Dotor-ina, Constable.

EFFING. Dotorina?

BUBBALOWE. Yes, our sous-chef. She just had major dental surgery. *(takes* **HONEY**'s *dishcloth and ties it around her face like a bandit)*

EFFING. Really?

BUBBALOWE. Yes, had half her teeth pulled out. They had to pump her full of laughing gas. What's going on in there *Dotorina?*

*(***HONEY*** laughs hysterically.)*

(From outside, we hear the sound of screeching brakes followed by several loud volleys of machine gun fire.)

AL. What the hell – ?

SHIRLEY. *(indicating the kitchen)* Sounds like it's comin' from the alley.

(There is another volley of machine gun fire.)

EFFING. Those are Tommy guns!

*(**AL** and **SHIRLEY** look at one another. **FRANK** enters from the kitchen.)*

FRANK. *(to **BUBBALOWE**)* It's a shootout! *(seeing **AL AND SHIRLEY**, switching to French accent)* I mean, eet eez a shootout! *(seeing **EFFING**, switching to Italian)* I mean-a, eetsa shootout!

EFFING. That must be Feghetti and his men. Everybody take cover!

(He rushes out through the kitchen. There is another loud volley of machine gun fire, very close by. Everybody ducks down.)

HONEY. *(grabbing **FRANK**'s hand, whispering)* Quick, in here!

*(**HONEY AND FRANK** run into the dining room.)*

SHIRLEY. That's gotta be Morris the Hound! Come on, Boss, we better see what's going on.

*(**AL** puts the bottle on the bar and he and **SHIRLEY** exit. There is a loud sound effect of light bulbs popping and flashes of light are seen through the archway.)*

BUBBALOWE. Oh my God! My neon sign!

*(He rushes out through the archway. The gunfight continues as **MICKEY** stirs, lifts his head up suddenly, looks around, shakes his head. Blackout.)*

End of Act One

ACT TWO

(A few moments later. All is quiet outside. **SHIRLEY** *enters cautiously through the archway, still in his whites, including the hat. His gun is drawn. He looks around the room, then creeps over to the basement door. He tries the door, finds it's locked. He crosses to the kitchen doors, pauses for a second, then throws his shoulder into one of them and disappears into the kitchen. At exactly the same time,* **AL** *comes flying out of the other kitchen door. He looks around quizzically, then goes back in through the same kitchen door as* **SHIRLEY** *comes out the other one.* **SHIRLEY** *looks around quizzically, shakes his head and exits into the dining room. He immediately appears backing in through the other dining room door as* **AL** *backs in from the kitchen. They bump into each other, scream, turn, and aim their guns at each other.)*

SHIRLEY. *(throwing up his hands)* Don't shoot, Boss, it's me!

AL. Geez, Shirley, I came this close to blowing your head off. I thought you was one of Morris the Hound's boys.

SHIRLEY. Nah, Morris' gang beat it out of here in a hurry. Once they seen our boys were here waitin' for 'em they took off like jack rabbits.

AL. Too bad they got away.

SHIRLEY. Still, that was some shoot-out, wasn't it?

AL. I dunno. I was stuck behind a garbage can the whole time. I couldn't see nuttin.'

SHIRLEY. Oh, it was great. You shoulda seen the faces on Morris's boys when they realized they'd walked right into an ambush!

AL. Serves 'em right for trying to hijack my booze. Any of our boys get hit?

SHIRLEY. I don't think so, Boss. They all scrammed when the cops arrived.

AL. Well, let's hope they made it over the border. Anyways, get me a drink, will ya? Gunfights always make me thirsty.

SHIRLEY. *(crossing to the punch and filling a glass)* Sure thing, Boss. *(notices* **MICKEY** *is gone)* Hey, what happened to Mickey?

(He peeks under the table.)

AL. I dunno. Plunkett musta stashed him somewhere.

SHIRLEY. I guess so.

(He hands **AL** *a glass of punch.)*

AL. *(gulping the whole thing down, then pulling a face)* Yeagghh! What are you trying to do – poison me?

SHIRLEY. Hey Boss, I know exactly what this stuff needs.

(He picks up the bottle of whiskey from the bar, opens it and starts pouring it into **AL***'s glass and then into the punch.)*

AL. *(sips)* That's more like it. So, looks like we'll have to get that shipment outta here by ourselves, huh Shirl?

SHIRLEY. Well there's a little problem with that, Boss. Our van got shot to pieces. They must have hit the gas tank or something. It went up like a Roman candle.

AL. They blew up my van? How the hell are we going to get that booze out of here without it?

*(***BUBBALOWE** *comes racing in from the archway.* **AL AND SHIRLEY** *whip around and point their guns at him.)*

BUBBALOWE. *(seeing them, throws his arms up)* Don't shoot, don't shoot!

AL. Oh it's you. *(lowering his gun)* What's going on out there, Plunkett?

BUBBALOWE. Nothing. It's all over. One minute it was like the Alamo, and the next everyone jumped in their cars and took off – with Effing following behind on his horse.

AL. Horse? Geez, don't they have cars in this country?

*(**HONEY** and **FRANK** come barrelling in from the kitchen. She is still a bit sooty, and carrying a dishcloth. She sees **BUBBALOWE**.)*

HONEY. *(with relief)* Oh, Pop!

AL. Pop?

*(**HONEY** turns and sees the gangsters, puts the dishcloth over her face again, and begins miming the gunfight.)*

HONEY. Er – pop! Pop! Bang! Bang! *(imitating a police siren)* Woo-OOO-ooo!

(she laughs hysterically, beat)

Wass ging gong?

AL. Huh? *(to **BUBBALOWE**)* What'd she say?

BUBBALOWE. I'm sorry, Dotorina doesn't speak much English.

FRANK. Dotorina?

BUBBALOWE. Yes. Our new sous-chef. She just arrived from... abroad.

AL. I can see she's a broad. Where's she from?

BUBBALOWE. Uh...

FRANK. Saskatchewan?

*(**BUBBALOWE** and **HONEY** exchange a look.)*

AL. Saskatchewan? I think I heard of that place. That's one of them desert countries, ain't it?

BUBBALOWE. *(relieved)* You could say that.

SHIRLEY. How does she do her job if she don't understand the lingo?

FRANK. Oh eet's not a problem, you see I speak a leetle... Saskatchewani.

SHIRLEY. Really? Where'd you learn that?

FRANK. *(improvising)* Well you know – when you have a singing career like mine, you peek up zees sings.

BUBBALOWE. That's right. In fact Maestro speaks a lot of languages. He's a polyglot.

SHIRLEY. Really? I thought he was a chef.

(FRANK and HONEY both react. AL turns to FRANK.)

AL. *(impressed)* So tell me LaPoof, what did she say just then?

FRANK. *(in his French accent)* Oh, er... she was just telling Monsieur Plunkett zat zee mousse is ready.

AL. Moose? I thought you was servin' goose.

FRANK. Non, non, you see, we start wiz zee mousse.

AL. Moose huh? I never tasted that before. What do you do with the antlers?

FRANK. Antlers? No, no, not zat kind of moose – *(using his hands as antlers)* – salmon mousse.

AL. *(still confused)* Salmon moose?

FRANK. Oui, eet's very delicious. I weel give you my recipe. Now, *(to* **HONEY,** *gesticulating wildly toward the kitchen door)* Dotorina, ngekht bakht een der kheetchmakh.

*(**HONEY** stares uncomprehendingly.)*

AL. What did you just say there?

FRANK. Oh, I was telleeng – Dotorina zat we must get back eento zee keetchen.

*(**HONEY,** finally understanding, nods and exits, muttering in gibberish as she goes.)*

Eet is time to prepare zee asparagoos.

AL. A pair of goose?

SHIRLEY. What happened to the moose?

FRANK. *(getting a tad impatient)* No, no. I tell you, zee goose is zee entrée. First we have zee mousse, zen we have zee goose, and zen we have zee asparagoos.

BUBBALOWE. Er, thank you, Maestro.

*(He shoves **FRANK** into the kitchen.)*

OK, let's get that hooch out of here before Effing gets back.

AL. We can't do that.

BUBBALOWE. What? Why not?

SHIRLEY. 'Cause our delivery truck's been shot to hell.

AL. Yeah, and my whole crew lammed it out of here.

BUBBALOWE. What are we going to do? I've got to get that stuff off the premises.

SHIRLEY. We're gonna need another set of wheels.

BUBBALOWE. What about the hearse?

SHIRLEY. The hearse! It was sittin' out there, right in the middle of that shootout.

AL. Come on, Shirl, we better go make sure it ain't been shot up as well.

SHIRLEY. Right.

(AL AND SHIRLEY head for the kitchen. AL stops and turns back.)

AL. Good thinkin', Plunkett.

BUBBALOWE. Thanks, Noodles.

AL. *(grabbing him by the collar)* That's Mr. Feghetti to you, pal.

BUBBALOWE. Whatever you say, Mr. Feghetti.

AL. *(letting him go)* Alright. Long as we got that straight. Let's go, Shirl.

(AL AND SHIRLEY exit into kitchen through one door as HONEY enters thru the other.)

HONEY. What are they doing, Pop?

BUBBALOWE. Planning their getaway.

HONEY. They're leaving? Thank goodness.

BUBBALOWE. Don't get too excited – they're not going anywhere yet. Not until they find some way of getting their booze out of here.

HONEY. Well, I don't know how much longer this Dotorina act is going to fool them.

(MICKEY walks in through the archway. HONEY and BUBBALOWE scream.)

BUBBALOWE. Mickey! You're alive!

(crossing to MICKEY kissing him on both cheeks)

Oh, thank God, thank God!

HONEY. This is incredible!

MICKEY. It is?

HONEY. Yes, I saw Feghetti shoot you right in the heart.

MICKEY. Right in the heart, eh? *(patting his heart)* Oh, what's this?

(He pulls the cigarette case out. It has a bullet lodged in it.)

BUBBALOWE. *(taking it from him)* Let me see that.

(He looks at it.)

Look at this, Honey. *(showing her the case)* The bullet from Noodles's .38. It's lodged right here in his cigarette case.

HONEY. Talk about your Lucky Strikes.

BUBBALOWE. *(turns to* **MICKEY***)* You lucky dog! Saved by a pack of cigarettes!

MICKEY. Cigarettes? Those things'll kill you, you know.

BUBBALOWE. I can't believe this! It's a miracle. Oh, I'm so glad you're alive.

MICKEY. You are?

BUBBALOWE. You bet. Because now I get to kill you myself!

(He grabs **MICKEY** *by the throat and proceeds to choke him.)*

You sonofabitch! How could you do this to me?

HONEY. Pop, Pop, take it easy. Come on, calm down.

BUBBALOWE. *(ignoring her)* Do you realize what you've done? Thanks to you, we're all going to get killed!

HONEY. *(intervening)* Pop! Stop it. You're only going to make things worse.

BUBBALOWE. Make a patsy out of me, will you?

HONEY. Pop, please –

BUBBALOWE. *(releasing him)* Now, here's what you're going to do, you little weasel: you're going to tell Noodles that I had nothing to do with this whole mess, you understand?

MICKEY. Noodles? Are we having noodles? With meatballs?

BUBBALOWE. Don't play games with me, Mickey.

MICKEY. I'm sorry. Have we met?

BUBBALOWE. What?

MICKEY. Do I know you?

BUBBALOWE. What are you trying to pull, Mickey?

MICKEY. Who's Mickey?

HONEY. You are.

MICKEY. I'm Mickey?

HONEY. Yes, Mickey McCall.

MICKEY. Mickey McCall. Hmm. Doesn't ring a bell. *(referring to his outfit)* Do I work in this place?

HONEY. Oh my goodness. He's lost his memory.

BUBBALOWE. How convenient.

HONEY. Oh Pop, show him a little sympathy. He's been through a terrible ordeal.

BUBBALOWE. Well whose fault is that? He brought it all on himself – and the rest of us.

HONEY. But we have to help him, he's in danger. I mean if the gangsters know he's alive they'll kill him. Again.

BUBBALOWE. You're right, they will.

(He starts for the kitchen.)

I'll just go and tell them he's here.

HONEY. *(grabbing his arm)* Pop! Be serious, you can't do that. You'd be an accessory to murder.

BUBBALOWE. According to Effing, I already am.

HONEY. Well here's your chance to save yourself. As long as Mickey's alive, you're in the clear. Come on, let's get him out of here.

BUBBALOWE. *(reluctantly)* Oh alright. *(turning to **MICKEY**)* But you're not off the hook yet, buddy.

MICKEY. Buddy? I thought I was Mickey.

HONEY. You are. Now look, you can't stay here. You're in a lot of danger.

MICKEY. I am?

HONEY. Yes. And it's very important that you get out of here right now – and that you don't come back.

MICKEY. Don't come back.

HONEY. That's right.

MICKEY. *(to* **BUBBALOWE***)* Where shall I go?

BUBBALOWE. *(irritably)* Who cares! *(shoving* **MICKEY** *toward the archway)* Why don't you go have a look at the Falls?

MICKEY. The Falls? *(excitedly)* You mean Niagara Falls? Wow, I've always wanted to go there.

*(***MICKEY** *exits.* **BUBBALOWE** *shakes his head.)*

BUBBALOWE. *(looking out after him)* With a bit of luck maybe he'll fall in.

*(***FRANK** *comes bustling in from the kitchen.)*

FRANK. I 'ave feenished zee mousse, I tought you might want to 'ave a look at eet.

BUBBALOWE. Oh, the mousse. Yes, of course. I'd love to.

(He exits into the kitchen. **FRANK** *watches him go and then pulls off his chef's hat, takes off* **BUBBALOWE***'s jacket, throws it into the closet and crosses to his suitcase.)*

HONEY. What are you doing?

FRANK. I'm getting out while I can.

(He heads for the archway. **HONEY** *runs after him and grabs his arm.)*

HONEY. What are you talking about? You can't leave now.

FRANK. I'm sorry Miss Bubbalowe, but I can't keep this up any longer. I mean, I don't know who the heck I am any more – or who anyone else is either. And in any case, I'm running out of accents.

HONEY. But you're doing so well!

FRANK. Yes, but what happens when Feghetti asks me to launch into an aria?

HONEY. Look, all Feghetti and Shirley care about is getting their booze out of here. They're not interested in you.

FRANK. You think they're just going to blow town and leave behind two witnesses to a murder? I don't think so.

HONEY. But there hasn't been any murder!

FRANK. What are you talking about?

HONEY. Mickey's still alive. He just walked out that door.

FRANK. He did?

HONEY. I saw him with my own eyes.

FRANK. You're kidding.

HONEY. So that murder we witnessed never took place.

FRANK. Well you know that and I know that, but do the gangsters know that?

HONEY. Look, forget about the gangsters. They're looking for Frankie Plunkett. As long as you're François LaPlouffe, you're safe.

FRANK. Oh no I'm not. If Immigration finds out I'm François LaPlouffe they're going to toss me in jail. And if the gangsters find out I'm Frank Plunkett, they're going to turn me into Swiss cheese. It's like going from the frying pan into the firing squad. I'm sorry, Miss Bubbalowe, but I'm leaving.

HONEY. What are you saying, Frank? That you're just going to abandon me?

FRANK. Oh, please don't put it like that.

HONEY. But that's what you're doing, isn't it – leaving me and my father in the lurch? I mean, who's going to cook the goose if you run out on us now?

FRANK. *(heading for the archway)* I'm sorry, Miss Bubbalowe but I've made up my mind. I'm leaving.

HONEY. Where are you going to go Frank? You said yourself you can't find a job.

FRANK. I can look after myself.

HONEY. And what about your poor sick mother back home? Who's going to look after her?

FRANK. I can't very well look after her if I'm dead, can I?

HONEY. But what are you going to do for money?

FRANK. I don't care about the money. I wouldn't stay here if you paid me a hundred bucks a week.

(**BUBBALOWE** *enters from the kitchen with a large platter of beautifully sculpted salmon mousse.*)

BUBBALOWE. *(impressed)* Oh Maestro! This is magnificent!

FRANK. *(no accent)* Look, Mr. Bubbalowe – there's something I have to tell you –

(**HONEY** *elbows him. He doubles over.*)

BUBBALOWE. *(focussed on the mousse)* You have truly outdone yourself. I cannot believe that with all that's been going on around here, you've managed to create something as breathtaking as this.

FRANK. But I'm not who you –

(**HONEY** *elbows him again. He doubles over.*)

BUBBALOWE. You know I have to admit, Maestro, I was a bit worried that I wouldn't be able to afford your salary; but one look at this mousse and I can see you're going to be worth every penny of that two hundred dollars a week!

(**FRANK** *drops the suitcase.*)

FRANK. *(stammering)* Two-hu – two hun – hun – hun –

HONEY. Was there something you wanted to say to my father, Monsieur LaPlouffe?

FRANK. Hm? Ah.

(French accent) Oui. I was just going to say – *(grabbing his hat and shoving it on his head)* I'd better get back to zee kitchen!

(**FRANK** *takes the mousse from* **BUBBALOWE.**)

BUBBALOWE. You go with him, Honey, before Noodles comes back. The less he sees of your face, the better.

(**AL** *and* **SHIRLEY** *enter from archway.*)

HONEY. Aagh!

(**BUBBALOWE**, *desperate, grabs* **HONEY** *by the back of the head and plunges her face into the mousse.* **FRANK** *moans.* **HONEY** *slowly lifts her head – she's covered in pink goo.)*

BUBBALOWE. *(turning to* **FRANK** *and* **HONEY,** *angrily)* You call this mousse? You should be ashamed of yourselves! Now get in there and start over again!

*(***FRANK*** and* ***HONEY*** head for the kitchen with the remains of the mousse.)*

And this time do it right!

*(***FRANK*** and* ***HONEY*** exit.* ***BUBBALOWE*** turns to the gangsters.)*

So hard to get good help these days. Anyway, what's the story with the hearse?

AL. It's gone.

BUBBALOWE. Gone? What do you mean?

SHIRLEY. Morris' boys musta stole it to make their getaway.

AL. Sonsabitches.

BUBBALOWE. You mean you're stuck here?

AL. For the time bein' – till we can find another set of wheels.

BUBBALOWE. Oh no! Now what do we do?

AL. At times like this there's only one thing to do.

*(***AL*** opens the closet door.)*

Abracadabra!

(He lifts one of the chef's hats on a shelf to reveal a bottle of whiskey.)

BUBBALOWE. So that's where you hid the stuff.

AL. Hey, who do you think you're dealin' with here, a couple o' rookies?

(He crosses back to the table, opens the bottle, and pours three large glasses of whiskey.)

BUBBALOWE. *(worried)* What are you doing?

AL. Take it easy, Plunkett. I'm just facilitatin' the thinkin' process. Here, have a snort.

(**SHIRLEY** *holds out a glass to* **BUBBALOWE** *who takes it, stares at the size of it.*)

BUBBALOWE. *(dubiously)* Thanks.

AL. *(holding out another glass)* Shirley?

SHIRLEY. *(as if this is completely normal)* Surely. Thanks, Boss.

(**AL** *holds up his glass.*)

AL. Well, down the hatch!

(They all clink glasses. **BUBBALOWE** *prepares himself. They're just about to drink when from the archway we hear –)*

VERONICA. *(off)* Hello?

SHIRLEY. Oh no! It's that lady cop again.

BUBBALOWE. Quick!

(They all turn and dump the contents of their drinks into the punch and set their glasses down.)

She's come back for LaPlouffe!

AL. What? Why?

BUBBALOWE. She wants to arrest him for being a Communist!

AL & SHIRLEY. COMMUNIST?

(**AL** *and* **SHIRLEY** *spit in unison.*)

BUBBALOWE. So if she asks if you've seen any French chefs around here –

AL. It's alright, Plunkett. We know what to do.

(**VERONICA** *enters upstage.* **AL** *hides the bottle behind his back.*)

VERONICA. Ah, Mr. Bubbalowe –

BUBBALOWE. *(forgetting himself)* Yes?

AL. *(incredulous)* Bubbalowe?

BUBBALOWE. Oh, I'm sorry, did you say Bubbalowe? I thought you said "Bubbaloni."

SHIRLEY. Bubbaloni? You said your name was Plunkett.

BUBBALOWE. Plunkett-Bubbaloni, actually – but the Bub-baloni's silent.

(AL and SHIRLEY look to one another.)

VERONICA. Plunkett-Bubbaloni?

BUBBALOWE. Yes. I'm Irish-Italian.

VERONICA. But aren't you the owner of this establishment?

BUBBALOWE. Who, me? Oh, no! That would be Mr. Bubba-lowe.

VERONICA. Well, I need to speak to him.

BUBBALOWE. I'm afraid he's indisposed.

SHIRLEY. Yeah, that's right. He decided to take the day off. For his health.

BUBBALOWE. Is there something I can help you with, Miss Snook?

VERONICA. Well Mr. uh –

BUBBALOWE. Plunkett –

(whispering the second part of the name very quickly out of the side of his mouth)

Bubbaloni. But please, call me Frank.

VERONICA. Alright, Frank. Has your chef LaPlouffe shown up yet?

BUBBALOWE. *(with a look to the gangsters)* No he hasn't. In fact he's not coming.

AL. *(helping)* That's right. Sorry, Miss Shnook. No French chefs here.

(FRANK enters from the kitchen, now wearing an apron and chef's hat, and carrying a bowl of fruit. He crosses to BUBBALOWE.)

FRANK. *(seeing the gangsters he immediately assumes his French accent)* Excusez-moi, Monsieur Bubb – er, Plunkett – where shall I put zee fruit bowl?

VERONICA. Aha! *(to AL)* No French chefs here, eh? *(crossing to FRANK, and taking the fruit bowl from him)* I'll take that, merçi beaucoup.

(She puts it on the bar.)

VERONICA. François LaPlouffe, you're under arrest for subversive activities.

FRANK. *(no accent)* Subversive activities?

VERONICA. That's right, you lousy Bolshevik.

FRANK. Bolshevik?

VERONICA. *(to FRANK)* You thought you'd given me the slip, eh? Well you're not getting away from me this time.

(VERONICA takes out a pair of handcuffs and slaps them on FRANK.)

BUBBALOWE. Please, Miss Snook, you can't take him away.

VERONICA. Not another word out of you, Mr. Plunkett – *(whispering out of the side of her mouth)* Bubbaloni, or I'll take you in for harbouring a fugitive.

(BUBBALOWE shrinks back.)

Wait till my supervisor finds out about this. Now he'll have to give me that promotion!

(HONEY, in her bandit get-up, races in from the kitchen, carrying a smoking saucepan.)

HONEY. Frunkh – dee shoush – dee –

(She sees FRANK's handcuffs. She lets out a scream and points at his handcuffs. She turns around and comes very close to AL. She lets out an even louder scream then covers it by laughing uproariously.)

VERONICA. And who might this be?

BUBBALOWE. Oh, I'm sorry. This is Dotorina, our sous-chef.

VERONICA. Indeed.

BUBBALOWE. I'm afraid she doesn't speak any English.

VERONICA. I see. Where's she from?

AL AND SHIRLEY. Saskatchewan.

VERONICA. *(sarcastically)* Of course she is. *(tapping HONEY on the shoulder)* Excuse me. If you're from Saskatchewan, I want to see a birth certificate.

HONEY. Huh?

VERONICA. *(loudly, over-enunciating each word)* Birth – certifi-cate. *(gesticulating as if playing charades)*) I – want – to – see – your – papers.

*(***HONEY*** *deliberately misinterpreting, starts to unbutton her top.)*

NO! Papers!

*(***HONEY*** *stares uncomprehendingly.)*

FRANK. Allow me. *(to* **HONEY**, *gesturing toward the archway)* Ngo oopshtars ungekt chor papyroos.

*(***HONEY*** *stares at him.)*

VERONICA. What did you just say?

AL. I think he just said go upstairs and get your papers.

FRANK. *(surprised)* That's right.

HONEY. Ah! Ikh wull goan geddem.

AL. *(pleased with himself)* Hey, I understood that too! She said she's gonna go and get 'em. I think I'm gettin' the hang of dis language!

BUBBALOWE. *(ushering her toward the archway)* Run along now, Dotorina.

HONEY. Khokee dokee.

*(***HONEY*** *exits thru the archway, laughing hysterically.)*

VERONICA. *(to* **FRANK***)* And her papers had better be in order, or I'm going to deport her along with you. *(quite suspicious, turning to* **AL AND SHIRLEY***)* Now what about you two? Where are you from? I suppose you're going to tell me you're just a couple of Jehovah's Witnesses.

SHIRLEY. No, no, not us. We never witnessed nuthin'.

AL. We was out of town.

VERONICA. I'm sorry, what did you say your name was?

*(***AL*** *and* **SHIRLEY** *look at* **BUBBALOWE***.)*

BUBBALOWE. *(indicating* **SHIRLEY***)* Oh, er, this is Mr. Humph-rey, the pastry chef. *(indicating* **AL***)* And this here's Mr. Dumphries –

AL. *(pouty)* The bus-boy.

BUBBALOWE. *(quickly)* They're Canadian, both of them.

VERONICA. *(disbelieving)* Canadian eh?

AL. *(going along with it)* That's right. Eh?

VERONICA. Alright then, if you're Canadian, you should be able to tell me the name of our Prime Minister.

(**AL** *and* **SHIRLEY** *look at each other.*)

AL. Prime Minister? I thought you guys had a king.

BUBBALOWE. *(quickly)* That's right! We did! McKenzie-King! He was our last prime minister, but –

VERONICA. Alright, Mr. Flunkit-Baloney or whatever your name is. *(crossing to the phone)* I think I've heard enough of this.

BUBBALOWE. What are you doing?

VERONICA. I'm calling our local office for reinforcements. This place is clearly full of illegals, and I'm going to need some help rounding them up.

BUBBALOWE. You can't do that!

VERONICA. *(dialling)* Oh yes I can. You ought to be ashamed of yourselves. There's a Depression going on, you know. Don't you realize these – undesirables – are taking food out of the mouths of honest Canadians?

BUBBALOWE. Miss Snook, please. This isn't what it looks like. You can't take Humpty and Dump – I mean Humphrey and Dumphries away – they're not undesirables – *(looking them up and down)* well, not in that sense –

VERONICA. I told you to be quiet. One more word and I'll take you and your cohorts and lock you all up in my paddy wagon.

(*At the mention of the paddy wagon,* **AL** *and* **SHIRLEY** *turn to* **VERONICA.**)

AL AND SHIRLEY. Paddy wagon?

VERONICA. Yes, that's what we use for transporting illegals.

AL. *(with a side-ways glance to* **SHIRLEY,** *crossing to* **VERONICA***)* Uh-huh. Is that so? Okay Miss Shnook, I'm gonna level with you. Me and Humpty here ain't Canadians. But you knew that right away, didn't you?

VERONICA. It was pretty obvious, I'm afraid. So where are you from?

AL. We're Americans.

VERONICA. Americans? Why didn't you just say so?

AL. The point is, the only illegals in this place are *(indicating* **FRANK***)* Frenchy here and that Dotty woman. They're the ones you want to lock up.

BUBBALOWE AND FRANK. *(protesting)* But, but – I – I – we – we –

SHIRLEY. Yeah, we been telling Mr. Bubbalowe for a long time that he shouldn't be hirin' foreigners, but he wouldn't pay no attention.

AL. *(He takes the phone from her and replaces the receiver.)* Listen, Miss Shnook, you don't need no back-up. You call in for reinforcements and you know what's gonna happen. They're gonna come in here and take over. Those nogoodniks are gonna get all the credit for your hard work and you'll be left out in the cold. Anyways, a smart cookie like you should be able to handle a situation like this single-handed.

VERONICA. *(flattered)* Do you really think so?

AL. Absolutely. If I was you I'd get upstairs right away. That Dotty woman ain't gonna hang around, now that she knows you're on to her. She's probably up there packin' her bags as we speak.

VERONICA. You're right. I better get up there.

(She unlocks one of **FRANK***'s handcuffs and cuffs him to the rail alongside of the bar.)*

VERONICA. *(cont.)* There, this ought to keep you safe till I get back. *(to the others)* Thanks for the tip, Mr. Dumpty. It's nice to know we can count on our American cousins for a helping hand.

AL. Hey. It's the least I can do.

(She smiles and exits through the archway. **AL** *waves at her.)*

(dropping his charm act, and putting the bottle he's been hiding down on the bar)

Okay, let's get down to business.

SHIRLEY. What the heck are you doin', Boss? We can't let her go, we're gonna need that paddy wagon.

BUBBALOWE. Yes, and why did you send her upstairs? She's going to take away my Hon – er – my daught – er – my Dotorina!

AL. Relax. I know what I'm doin.' She ain't gonna take away nobody. Now get upstairs, Shirl, and make sure Miss Shnook don't come back down.

SHIRLEY. Right, Boss.

BUBBALOWE. WHAT?

AL. *(ignoring* **BUBBALOWE***)* And Shirl?

SHIRLEY. Yes, Boss?

AL. Go easy, okay?

*(**SHIRLEY** exits through the archway.)*

BUBBALOWE. He's not going to hurt her, is he?

AL. Don't ask so many questions, Plunkett. Now get down in the basement and start haulin' up that booze. I'll bring that paddy wagon round to the kitchen door and we can start loading it up.

*(**BUBBALOWE** crosses to the basement door and unlocks it with his keys.)*

AL. *(to* **FRANK***)* You, La Poof, give us a hand.

FRANK. *(waving his unshackled hand, with French accent)* Well, I'm afraid one 'and is all I can give you.

AL. Oh, right. I forgot about that.

(He pulls out his gun and shoots **FRANK**'s *handcuff free.* **FRANK** *screams as* **AL** *crosses to the archway.)*

(turning back) Now get to work.

(He exits.)

FRANK. *(counting his fingers)* One, two, three, four, five – oh thank God.

*(He promptly faints. **BUBBALOWE** catches him before he hits the ground.)*

BUBBALOWE. *(slapping **FRANK**'s cheeks)* Monsieur LaPlouffe, are you okay? Maestro?

*(He picks up the bottle on the bar and pours the remaining sip or two into **FRANK**'s mouth. **FRANK** sputters, but comes to.)*

FRANK. Hey, that's good stuff.

(He reaches for the bottle.)

BUBBALOWE. Sorry Monsieur, this isn't the time.

*(**BUBBALOWE** grabs it from him and tosses it down the chute.)*

(steering him to the basement door) Now we'd better do what Noodles says. You go down and start bringing up that pea soup and I'll get the stuff out of the closet.

*(**FRANK** exits into the basement. **BUBBALOWE** crosses to the closet, opens the door and pulls out the box which Effing examined earlier. It is heavy and contains lots of cans. He takes out some cans and puts them back on the shelf in the closet. He then removes the chef's hats that are still sitting on the shelf, revealing the bottles hidden underneath. He starts to pack them into the box as **HONEY** comes running in from the archway, wearing an evening dress, and sunglasses.)*

BUBBALOWE. Honey! Thank God you're alright. *(seeing her outfit, with alarm)* Why are you dressed like that? What happened to your disguise?

HONEY. I had to ditch Dotorina before she got deported to Saskatchewan. *(looking at her watch)* Oh my God. *(picking up the pot she'd brought in earlier)* I better get back in the kitchen and see how things are going.

BUBBALOWE. No! You can't go in there. Noodles will be coming through there any second.

HONEY. But Pop, people are going to start arriving soon. What about the dinner?

BUBBALOWE. *(loading her up with linens from the closet)* You let me worry about that. Stay in the dining room for now. You can finish setting up in there.

(He grabs the fruit bowl and puts it on top of her pile of linens.)

Here – this is the centerpiece for the buffet table. Now whatever you do, stay out of sight.

*(**SHIRLEY** enters from the archway and **AL** comes in from the kitchen. **BUBBALOWE** pushes **HONEY** into the closet with the fruitbowl and closes the door.)*

AL. Okay, we're ready to go out there. Everything taken care of?

SHIRLEY. Sure is, Boss.

AL. Good. Let's get movin.'

*(to **BUBBALOWE**)* What are you doing standing there, Plunkett? Make yourself useful.

BUBBALOWE. I was just getting the bottles out of the closet.

*(He crosses to the boxes and closes them up as **FRANK** enters from the basement carrying a stack of boxes that are much too heavy for him. He staggers under their weight.)*

FRANK. He-e-elp!

SHIRLEY. Gimme those, LaPoof.

*(**SHIRLEY** crosses to him and takes the boxes as if they weigh nothing. He exits through the kitchen.)*

AL. Geez LaPoof, all that French cookin' ain't done much for your stamina, has it? You oughta ease up on those mooses and gooses and try a good steak once in a while.

FRANK. Maybe you're right, Monsieur.

AL. *(coming right up to him)* You know, I'm disappointed in you, LaPoof. I'd never have pegged you for a Commie.

(**AL** *exits into the basement.*)

FRANK. Commie?

BUBBALOWE. Come on Maestro, we better get cracking.

FRANK. But Monsieur! What do I do about zee dinner? I cannot be a chef and a stock-boy at zee same time. If I don't get some 'elp, I'm never going to feenish!

BUBBALOWE. *(picking up the boxes and heading towards the kitchen)* I apologize, Monsieur LaPlouffe. But I promise you, as soon as we get this stuff out of here, you'll have all the help you need.

(**BUBBALOWE** *exits into the kitchen.*)

FRANK. *(noticing one last bottle on the floor)* Monsieur Bubba-Plunkett – you missed one. *(examining the label, no accent)* V.S.O.P.

(*He opens the bottle and takes a healthy swig.*)

Hmm! It'd be a shame to waste this.

(*He looks down at the punch bowl.*)

Why not? Couldn't hurt.

(*He begins to empty the bottle into it. Suddenly we hear* **EFFING**'s *voice.*)

EFFING. *(off)* BUBBALOWE!!

(**FRANK** *starts and looks around in a panic.*)

(*shaking the bottle*) Come on, come on!

(*He gives up, races over to the chute and tosses the bottle down it.* **EFFING** *enters from the archway. He looks as though he's been through a war. His hat is crooked, one sleeve of his tunic is coming loose, his jodhpurs are torn and soiled when he turns around, we see a large rip in the seat of his pants.*)

EFFING. Ah, Signor Pagliacci. You're still here.

FRANK. Pagliacci? *(Italian accent)* Oh, oui – I mean, si.

EFFING. Where's Bubbalowe?

FRANK. He's a-gone.

EFFING. Gone? Gone where?

FRANK. To de church.

EFFING. Church?

FRANK. To see about Mama's a-funeral. He's a-gone-a to see de priest.

EFFING. He's going to need a priest by the time I'm done with him.

FRANK. Maybe you should-a come back-a later, Signor.

EFFING. I'm not going anywhere. There's contraband liquor in here somewhere, and I'm going to search this place from top to toe until I find it.

FRANK. *(thinking madly)* Liquor eh? Well, now dat you mention it, I tink I saw some-a boxes in-a de dining room.

EFFING. The dining room eh? I'll have a look.

(He starts toward the dining room.)

FRANK. Very good. Now, if you'll excuse-a-me, Signor Effing, I 'ave-a to check my oven.

EFFING. Oven?

FRANK. Si. To see if de goose she is-a cooked.

EFFING. Goose? I thought you were the undertaker.

FRANK. *(catching himself)* Oh. Si. Dat's what Signor Bubba-lowe called his-a Mama. De old-a goose.

EFFING. What do you mean you have to see if she's cooked?

FRANK. *(madly thinking)* Well – er – you see – de family 'as decided on-a cremation.

EFFING. *(reacts)* I see. Remind me never to eat in this restaurant.

*(He exits into the dining room. **SHIRLEY** and **BUBBA-LOWE** enter from the kitchen as **AL** comes in from the basement laden with boxes.)*

SHIRLEY. Boss, that Mountie's back. I just seen his horse.

FRANK. *(Italian then French accent)* Si! I mean, oui! 'Ee's in zee dining room.

(He indicates the dining room.)

AL. *(crossing toward the kitchen door)* Damn. I thought we were rid of that Effing clown. I better dump this stuff. Lock that door, Plunkett, I don't want him snoopin' around my hooch.

(**AL** *exits into the kitchen.*)

BUBBALOWE. *(locking the basement door and pocketing the key)* You and me both. Okay, you two, you better disappear while I figure out a way to get rid of him.

(**EFFING** *enters from the dining room.* **BUBBALOWE** *and* **FRANK** *dive behind the bar.* **SHIRLEY** *is caught in the open.*)

EFFING. Ah, Mr. Humphrey, good. I was wondering where everybody was.

SHIRLEY. What happened to you?

EFFING. Eh? *(looking down at himself)* Oh. Rosie threw me.

SHIRLEY. Really? She must be one tough broad.

EFFING. What are you talking about? Rosie's my horse.

SHIRLEY. Oh.

(**AL** *enters from the kitchen.*)

AL. Hey Shirley –

EFFING. Shirley?

AL. *(seeing* **EFFING***)* Uh, surely you have something to do in the kitchen, Humpty? Why don't you get in there and sweep the floor?

SHIRLEY. *(snatching the cigar from* **AL***'s mouth)* That's Mr. Humpty to you, Dumpty; and I'm the one who gives the orders around here, don't forget. Now, YOU get in there an' sweep the floor!

AL. What?

SHIRLEY. You heard me.

(indicating closet door) Grab yourself a broom and hop to it.

(**AL** *glares at* **SHIRLEY** *who grins and opens the closet door.* **HONEY** *comes out. She still wears her sunglasses and has arranged the basket of fruit on her head as a headdress,*

tied under her chin with napkins. She smiles nonchalantly,
sees **AL** *and* **SHIRLEY** *and swallows loudly.)*

HONEY. Buenos dias.

EFFING. And who are you?

HONEY. *(in a pseudo-Spanish accent, complete with a Castillian*
lisp) Uh, how do joo do? I'm Maria Calamara Ensalada
Tequila – de Barcelona. *(with a look to the gangsters)* Dee
dancer.

(She makes a pathetic attempt at a few Flamenco steps,
clicking her fingers like castanets.)

EFFING. What were you doing in the closet?

HONEY. Dee closet? Oh, I thought it was dee ladies' room!

EFFING. *(suspicious)* Ladies room? Step aside please, Miss. I
need to have a look around in there.

HONEY. What are joo looking for?

EFFING. Contraband.

HONEY. Contra-who?

EFFING. Alcohol. I know Bubbalowe's hiding a shipment of
it here somewhere. *(seeing* **AL** *and* **SHIRLEY***)* What are
you two looking at? Don't you have something better
to do?

SHIRLEY. Uh, yeah. Actually, I should get back to my, uh –
peach clafouti. C'mon, Dumpty.

*(***AL*** *and* **SHIRLEY** *exit into the kitchen.)*

EFFING. *(to* **HONEY***)* Excuse me.

(He goes into the closet. **BUBBALOWE** *pops up from*
behind the bar. He hisses at **HONEY** *and indicates for*
her to shut the door. She sees this, quickly shuts the closet
door and puts her weight against it.)

FRANK. *(popping up, French accent)* I cannot work like zees.
My kitchen is like Union Station. Any more distrac-
tions and zee dinner she will be ruined!

BUBBALOWE. *(to* **FRANK***)* I'm so sorry Maestro.

FRANK. I cannot create under zees conditions! I am an
artiste – I need to concentrate.

BUBBALOWE. Of course, Maestro. You're absolutely right. Now, let's get you back in the kitchen. *(to* **HONEY***)* And you – er – Señorita – get back into the dining room and finish setting up.

*(***MICKEY*** enters from the archway.)*

MICKEY. Excuse me.

BUBBALOWE. Oh no, not again.

HONEY. Mickey!

MICKEY. *(offering his hand)* How do you do, Mickey.

HONEY. No, YOU'RE Mickey!

MICKEY. I am? I'm sorry, have we met?

BUBBALOWE. How many times do I have to tell you? You're going to get yourself killed. Now, get out of here!

(shoving **MICKEY** *toward the archway)*

Go back to the Falls!

MICKEY. *(excited)* The Falls?

BUBBALOWE. Yes.

MICKEY. You mean Niagara Falls?

BUBBALOWE. Yes!

MICKEY. *(as he exits)* Wow! I've always wanted to go there.

(The closet door is pushed open and **HONEY** *is propelled into the dining room.* **EFFING** *steps into the room.)*

EFFING. Ah, Bubbalowe, you're back from church, I see.

BUBBALOWE. Church?

(He looks at **FRANK***, who shrugs.)*

EFFING. Don't mess with me, Bubbalowe. I've had a hard day. Now, where have you hidden that liquor?

BUBBALOWE. I don't know what you're talking about.

EFFING. *(his impatience building)* Oh, don't give me that. It's here somewhere. Now, you and I are going to have a little look around – starting with that basement.

FRANK. *(adopting his Italian accent)* 'Scuza me Signor, I musta be getting on with de uh – preparations.

BUBBALOWE. Sure, sure, go right ahead.

(**FRANK** *exits into the kitchen.*)

EFFING. Alright now, Bubbalowe –

BUBBALOWE. Listen, Constable Effing, I'd love to be able to help you but as you can see this really isn't the time. I have sixty guests arriving for a dinner party any minute now, I'm very short-handed in the kitchen and to top it all off, I've just gone and lost my mother!

EFFING. (*sarcastically*) Oh that's right – the "old goose." What kind of idiot do you think you're dealing with here Bubbalowe?

BUBBALOWE. Is this a trick question?

(**EFFING** *tries the basement door and finds it's locked.*)

EFFING. This door is locked.

BUBBALOWE. It is?

EFFING. Alright Bubbalowe, quit stalling and give me the key to this door.

BUBBALOWE. (*putting his hands in his pockets and pretending to search*) The key? Oh, the key. Sorry. Must have left it in my other pants.

EFFING. Alright, if you want to do it the hard way, that's fine with me. I'll just shoot the lock off.

(*He pulls out his gun.*)

BUBBALOWE. (*blocking the doorway*) No, please!!

EFFING. (*taking aim*) Move away from the door.

(*He does, plugging his ears.* **EFFING** *tries to shoot. The gun jams.*)

(*livid*) Gol-DARN IT!

(*He fiddles with the gun, tries again. Nothing.*)

You lousy son of a gun.

(*He slams the gun down on the bar. It goes off with a loud bang.* **EFFING**'s *hat flies in the air. He and* **BUBBALOWE** *jump.*)

EFFING & BUBBALOWE. AAGH!

(**EFFING** *picks up his hat and pokes his finger through the hole he's just shot in it.*)

EFFING. *(livid)* Now look what you made me do!! *(throws it down)* Alright, Bubbalowe, open that door right now, or I'm going to break it down.

BUBBALOWE. *(pleading)* Constable, please. I just renovated!

EFFING. Out of my way!

(*He runs at the door, screaming.* **BUBBALOWE** *scoots out of the way.* **EFFING** *hurls himself against the door. Nothing happens. Beat.*)

Ow.

(*He turns, furious.*)

BUBBALOWE. *(stepping toward him, concerned)* Are you alright?

EFFING. Get away from me, Bubbalowe. I've had enough of your shenanigans for one day. I'm going to get into that basement if it kills me!

(*He spots the chute.*)

Aha!

(*He crosses to it and opens the chute door, tests its strength, then starts to climb into the chute feet first.*)

BUBBALOWE. What are you doing?

(*crossing to him*)

You can't go down there like that!

EFFING. Oh no? Just watch me.

(*He slides down the chute. The door slams shut behind him, and* **BUBBALOWE** *immediately yanks it open. We hear a long, protracted scream, followed by a series of loud crashes, some glass tinkling, then silence. A beat.*)

BUBBALOWE. *(calling down the chute in a very small voice)* Constable Effing?…

(*Beat. Then, with mounting trepidation*)

Constable Effing? *(wailing in panic)* Constable Effing!! Ohmygod ohmygod ohmygod…

(He then rushes over to the basement door, unlocks it and exits down the stairs, leaving the door open.)

BUBBALOWE. *(cont.) (off)* Constable Effing!

(AL AND SHIRLEY enter into the archway, one on either side, guns drawn. They peek into the room and see that it is apparently empty.)

SHIRLEY. Looks like the coast is clear.

(They come in.)

AL. Coulda sworn I heard a shot.

SHIRLEY. *(picking up EFFING's hat off the bar)* Hey, look at this, Boss. *(wiggling his finger through the hole)* Bullet hole.

AL. *(picking up EFFING's gun)* Looks like Plunkett tried to give that Effing Mountie a haircut.

BUBBALOWE. *(wailing, off)* Oh my God!

(AL AND SHIRLEY raise their weapons and turn to the basement door, as BUBBALOWE comes running in, distraught.)

I killed him! He's dead!

AL. *(handing him EFFING's revolver)* Nice shootin', Plunkett. I didn't know you had it in you.

BUBBALOWE. *(putting the gun back down on the bar)* No, you don't understand. I didn't shoot him. He went down the chute!

(AL AND SHIRLEY look at each other, perplexed.)

SHIRLEY. I'm confused.

BUBBALOWE. Look, it doesn't matter. The fact is, I killed a Mountie! He's lying down there on the basement floor!

AL. Well however you did it, I'm proud of yous. Come on Shirl, now's our chance to clean the rest of that hooch out of there.

(AL AND SHIRLEY exit into the basement.)

BUBBALOWE. *(looking after AL and SHIRLEY as they go)* I can't believe this is happening. This morning I was just a regular guy, with a regular life, trying to open a regular restaurant, now suddenly I'm a rum-running, gun-toting, Mountie-murdering mobster!

HONEY. *(entering from the dining room, still disguised as Carmella)* Is everything alright, Pop?

BUBBALOWE. *(turning on her)* Fine! Wonderful! Hunky dory!

HONEY. *(a little thrown by his outburst)* Well, I just wanted to let you know the dining room's ready.

BUBBALOWE. Who cares about the dining room? The only dining room I'll be seeing from now on is the one in Kingston Penitentiary – that is, assuming they don't just hang me!

HONEY. Hang you? What are you talking about?

*(**MICKEY** enters through the archway.)*

MICKEY. Excuse me.

BUBBALOWE. For Heaven's sake!

HONEY. Not now, Mickey.

MICKEY. *(crossing into the room)* I'm sorry to bother you, but I –

BUBBALOWE. Mickey, once and for all, get it through your head – you can't keep coming back here. If Noodles sees your face, he'll kill you!

*(**AL AND SHIRLEY** enter from the basement, carrying boxes. **HONEY** and **BUBBALOWE** scream, turn **MICKEY** and push him toward the kitchen. At the same time, **FRANK**, carrying a smaller but equally well-sculpted salmon mousse, enters from the kitchen.)*

FRANK. Monsieur Plunka – Bubba – AAGH!

*(**MICKEY** ends up face-first in the mousse. He lifts his head, slowly. **FRANK** bursts into tears.)*

BUBBALOWE. *(mortified)* Oh, Maestro, I'm so sorry.

FRANK. *(whimpering)* My mousse, my mousse!

BUBBALOWE. *(turning to **MICKEY**)* You idiot! Now look what you've done. That's it, you're fired. Get out of here – and stay out.

(He propels him toward the archway.)

BUBBALOWE. *(cont.)* *(shouting after him)* And don't come back!

*(**MICKEY** exits. **BUBBALOWE** turns to **FRANK**.)*

Well, Maestro, I guess the mousse is off. Can you do anything with pea soup?

*(**FRANK** looks at him and then bursts into tears again. **MICKEY** re-enters, his face covered in pink goo.)*

MICKEY. Excuse me, where was I going again?

BUBBALOWE, FRANK and **HONEY.** NIAGARA FALLS!

MICKEY. *(excited)* Oh good!

(as he exits) I've always wanted to go there.

*(**SHIRLEY** dips a finger into the remains of the mousse and has a taste.)*

SHIRLEY. It's good but it's not the best.

*(**FRANK** slaps his hand.)*

FRANK. *(French accent)* Keep your mitts off my mousse, Monsieur. *(stifling a sob)* I'll be in zee kitchen.

(He exits.)

HONEY. *(Spanish accent)* I will go and do some e-stretches.

(She heads for the dining room.)

AL. Hey you. Wait a minute.

HONEY. *(nervous)* Hoo, me?

AL. Yeah, what was your name again, honey?

HONEY. Huh?

*(**HONEY AND BUBBALOWE** look at each other.)*

(trying to remember) Oh. Uh, Maria Fritata Paella Tortilla – *(suddenly remembering)* De Barcelona.

AL. You know, you look awful familiar.

BUBBALOWE. *(taking a box or two from **AL**)* Here, Mr. Feghetti, let me help you with those. You go and do a few pirou-ettes, Señorita – er – Fajita. I'll be right back.

*(**AL, SHIRLEY** and **BUBBALOWE** exit into the kitchen. **HONEY** is heaving a sigh of relief when suddenly*

EFFING *bursts in from downstairs, a bottle of booze in his hand. He's in very rough shape, a bit dazed and limping.)*

EFFING. *(seeing* **HONEY***)* Ah, Miss Barcelona.

(holding his head) Ouch. I think I need to sit down.

HONEY. *(steering him to a chair)* Of course. Let me help joo.

(She sits him down.)

(reaching for the bottle)

Here, I'll take dat.

EFFING. *(hanging on to it)* No, no, no! That's my evidence!

HONEY. *(gently prying it from his hands)* I theenk you've had enough eveedence for one day.

EFFING. I don't feel so good.

HONEY. Here, let me get joo some punch.

EFFING. Good idea. I'm dying of thirst.

(She sets the bottle on the table and starts to pour a glass for **EFFING***. He reaches over, picks up the entire bowl and proceeds to guzzle the contents.)*

HONEY. *(archly)* Help joorself.

EFFING. *(setting down the bowl of punch)* This has not been my day, you know.

HONEY. *(offering Effing a glass of punch)* Why do joo say dat? What has happened?

EFFING. What hasn't happened? I was supposed to get my corporal's stripes today. Instead I've been shot at, thrown from my horse, thwarted by a bunch of thugs and rendered unconscious in a basement full of booze!

HONEY. Oh my goodness. Joo poor man.

EFFING. But it hasn't been in vain.

(taking the glass of punch from **HONEY***)*

No siree.

(indicating the bottle on the table)

Because I've got all the evidence I need now to put that crook Bubbalowe behind bars!

HONEY. Señor Bubbalowe? A crook? I don't believe it. I know heem very well. He would never do anytheeng wrong. He ees a very honest hombre.

(EFFING finishes his glass of punch.)

EFFING. You know, this stuff really hits the spot. I think I'll have another.

(He pours another glass. We hear a horse's whinny from offstage.)

Oh my God. Rosie!

HONEY. Hoo?

EFFING. Rosie, my horse. She hasn't had any water for hours. She must be parched!

(He tries to stand, is overcome by a wave of dizziness.)

(sitting again) Ooh.

HONEY. Don' try to move. Joo just sit right there and relax. I will get Rosie some water, OK?

EFFING. That's very kind of you. *(hiccupping)* Excuse me.

(She exits thru the archway. **EFFING** *helps himself to more punch.)*

Don't know why I'm so thirsty all of a sudden. Must be all this ekshershise. *(He thinks.)* Ex-er-cise.

(He hiccups again, then drinks his punch. He looks around, blearily, and tries to get up. He loses his balance, tips the chair over with a crash, and lands on the floor on his backside. **AL** *enters from the kitchen and sees* **EFFING** *on the floor.)*

AL. What are you doin' here? I thought you was dead.

EFFING. There's something wrong with this chair.

(standing unsteadily)

Alright, Mr. Dumpty, I've had it with puttyfoossing around. Where'd he go?

(calling) Bubbalowe!

AL. Bubbalowe? He ain't here. He's been gone all day.

EFFING. No he hasn't. He's right here. I was just talking to him.

AL. Is that a fact?

EFFING. Yes. *(pouring himself some more punch)* You should try this punch. It's good stuff, you know.

*(**BUBBALOWE** enters from the kitchen, sees **EFFING** apparently still alive, and is thrilled.)*

BUBBALOWE. Constable Effing! Thank God. Boy am I glad to see you!

EFFING. Not half as glad as I am to see you.

(He tries to stand, winds up on his butt.)

You've got to get that chair fixed. Alright, Buster –

*(crawling to **BUBBALOWE** on his hands and knees and grabbing him by the ankle)*

I've got you now, and this time I'm not letting go.

*(He pulls himself up, using **BUBBALOWE**'s body as leverage, then gets out his handcuffs.)*

Hold out your hands. You're under arrest!

*(As he lifts the handcuffs to slap them on **BUBBALOWE**'s wrist, he passes out. **AL** catches him from behind.)*

BUBBALOWE. *(slapping **EFFING**'s wrists and cheeks)* Constable? Constable Effing? Oh no, now he really is dead!

AL. Naw, he ain't dead. Just dead drunk.

*(**EFFING** snores loudly. **AL** sits him in the chair downstage right. **EFFING** cuddles up to **AL**. **AL** extricates himself.)*

BUBBALOWE. *(dumbfounded)* Drunk?

AL. *(picking up the bottle from the table)* Yeah, looks like he's been helpin' himself to my hooch.

BUBBALOWE. Effing? He's a teetotaler!

AL. He's totalled now. Anyway, he just tole me Bubbalowe's here.

BUBBALOWE. He what?

AL. Yeah. He says he's been here all day.

BUBBALOWE. *(panicked)* He has?

AL. Now I can get my hooch and get even with that fink Bubbalowe all at the same time!

BUBBALOWE. *(forcing a pained smile on his face)* Good for you. Well, we'd better get moving before he wakes up.

AL. Right.

> *(AL and BUBBALOWE exit into the basement. VERONICA enters thru the archway, looking extremely dishevelled. Her hair is down, her dress is in tatters, her stockings are torn, and she's minus a heel on one shoe.)*

VERONICA. Oh, excuse me!

EFFING. *(waking with a start)* Hello. Who are you?

VERONICA. Thank God, a policeman! You've got to help me, Constable. I've just been upstairs in the lavatory for the last hour!

EFFING. An hour, eh? You don't need a policeman, you need a doctor.

VERONICA. No, you don't understand – I was locked in there against my will! Mr. Humpty knocked me on the head and stuffed me in there. When I came to, I managed to pry open the window and crawl out to the fire escape. I nearly broke my ankle going down those stairs.

EFFING. *(fumbling for his notebook and pencil)* Sounds serious. I'd better file a report. Could I get your name?

VERONICA. Veronica Snook. I'm with the Immigration branch.

EFFING. How do you do, Miss Snook? I apologize for not standing, but I'm feeling a little – woozy just now.

VERONICA. You and me both.

EFFING. Well don't you worry Miss Shnook, I'll take care of everything.

> *(offering his hand, missing hers a couple of times before finally grasping it and shaking hands)*

I'm Hamilton Xavier Effing, Croyal Manadian – Royal Panadian – I'm a Mountie. *(looking at her a little more closely)* You look like you've really been through the wringer.

VERONICA. Please excuse my appearance. I tore my dress climbing out the window.

(She tries to cover the holes in her dress with her hands.)

EFFING. *(earnestly)* Don't give it another thought. I think you look delightful.

VERONICA. You do?

EFFING. Please, have a seat. Help yourself to a glass of fruit punch. It's good stuff. It'll perk you right up.

VERONICA. Really?

EFFING. Sure. It worked for me.

(He falls off his chair onto his backside.)

Oops. Pardon me.

(He crawls back onto his chair.)

VERONICA. *(pouring herself a glass and then offering him some)* Well if you say so. Here, may I top you up?

EFFING. *(holding out his glass)* Thank you. So, what's an attractive woman like you doing in a dreary place like Immigration? I would have pegged you for a movie star.

VERONICA. *(flattered)* Oh, go on! You're just saying that.

EFFING. *(stifling a yawn)* No, I mean it.

(VERONICA drinks her punch and reacts to it. Meanwhile, AL appears at the basement door, sees EFFING and VERONICA, retreats slightly and eavesdrops on the following.)

VERONICA. Wow! That stuff's really got a kick to it, hasn't it?

EFFING. *(pouring another glass)* Here, have some more.

VERONICA. Thanks.

EFFING. Now, Vernonica – Veronana – *(taking another stab at it)* Veronanonanon – *(lost in the intricacies of the name)* anonanonanon – do you mind if I call you Nonnie?

VERONICA. No, not at all. I've always wanted someone to call me that.

EFFING. *(yawning again)* So, you didn't answer my question – what's a beautiful girl like you doing working for the government?

VERONICA. Beautiful? Oh, go on. I'm not beautiful.

EFFING. *(emphatically)* You are too. And don't let anyone tell you any different.

VERONICA. Why, thank you, Constable. Well the truth is, I never expected to make a career of government work. I always thought I'd be married and settled by now. I guess I just never found Mr. Right.

EFFING. *(moved to tears)* Oh, Nonnie, that's so sad.

VERONICA. Isn't it? I get so dreadfully lonely sometimes. I mean, my work keeps me busy and all, but I'd give it up in an instant if I could only find the right man.

EFFING. *(stifling a yawn)* Would you really?

VERONICA. Oh yes. And it's not as though I'm asking for that much. I mean, I'm not looking for Clark Gable or anything. All I want is someone who really appreciates me for who I am.

AL. *(reacting to this)* Huh!

(AL quickly disappears, closing the basement door. VERONICA turns to see what the noise was.)

VERONICA. What was that?

(She shrugs, turns back to EFFING.)

Anyway, I'm awfully sorry, I shouldn't be boring you with all of this, Constable.

EFFING. *(blearily)* Not at all. I'm enjoying it. And please, call me Hammy.

VERONICA. *(touched)* Thank you, Hammy. Here, let me pour you another glass of punch.

EFFING. *(having difficulty staying awake)* Mm.

(She stands and refills both their glasses.)

VERONICA. *(raising a glass)* Well, here's to new friends!

EFFING. *(waving his glass about unsteadily)* To nw frnds.

(They clink glasses and drink. EFFING sets his glass down. She turns away to do likewise as EFFING begins to keel over. She turns back just as EFFING falls face first into her bosom.)

VERONICA. Constable Effing! What are you doing?

EFFING. *(lifting his head momentarily and looking at her)* Oh darling, it's been so long! Mmf.

(He falls into her bosom again.)

VERONICA. It certainly has! Oh what the hell? You only live once. *(downing her drink and throwing her arms out in submission)* Take me, Hammy – I'm all yours!

*(She wraps her arms around him. Beat. We hear **EFFING** snoring loudly.)*

Constable?

(no response)

Constable Effing?

(still nothing)

Hammy?

*(She shakes him. He snores on. He is holding on to her dress. As she pushes him back into his chair and steps away, her dress comes off in **EFFING**'s hands. He wraps it under his chin like a blanket. She is left in her slip.)*

VERONICA. AAGH!!

(She looks around to check if anyone can see her.)

Oh my God. *(tugging at her dress)* Hammy, please! I need my dress!

*(She tugs at it again. He pushes her away, turns on his side and hugs the dress tighter. The basement door opens. **VERONICA** looks down at herself, panics, looks around, sees the closet door, and exits into it. **AL** peeks in from the basement door. **EFFING** snores loudly. Satisfied, **AL** enters.)*

AL. OK, Plunkett, the coast is clear.

*(**BUBBALOWE** staggers in from the basement, loaded down with some boxes. **SHIRLEY** and **FRANK** enter from the kitchen, arguing heatedly.)*

SHIRLEY. Hey La Poof, all I'm saying is, you better baste that Goose Guillotine, it's looking a little dry.

FRANK. *(French accent)* It's not Goose Guillotine! It's Gallantine, you imbecile. GALLANTINE!!

BUBBALOWE. Maestro please! We have no time to lose! Effing could wake up any second. *(handing his boxes to* **SHIRLEY***)* Here – take these.

SHIRLEY. *(taking them)* Okay, but somebody better baste that goose…

> *(***SHIRLEY*** *and* **AL** *exit into kitchen.)*

FRANK. *(French accent)* I can't work like zees! One minute I'm supposed to be cremating Mother Goose, and the next I'm getting cooking lessons from John Dillinger!

> *(***HONEY*** *enters thru the archway, her headdress is pretty much gone. She clutches a half-eaten banana.)*

BUBBALOWE. *(seeing the headdress)* Honey. Where have you been? What happened to your disguise?

HONEY. Effing's horse ate it.

BUBBALOWE. Ask a silly question…

> *(***AL*** *and* **SHIRLEY** *enter from the kitchen. They come face to face with* **HONEY***.)*

AL. Hey, look Shirley, it's Chiquita Banana.

SHIRLEY. What happened to your outfit?

HONEY. *(Spanish accent)* Oh, uh, I was hungry.

> *(She takes a bite of banana and smiles.)*

AL. You know, I could swear I seen you somewhere before.

BUBBALOWE. I don't think so. Listen Noodles, we really don't have time for thi –

AL. *(grabbing* **BUBBALOWE** *by the throat)* I told you before. NOBODY calls me Noodles. Get it?

BUBBALOWE. I'm sorry Mr. Feghetti, I feghetti. I forgotti. I forgot!

AL. *(to* **HONEY***)* Now come here a minute, sweetie.

> *(She hesitates, looks to* **BUBBALOWE***.)*

Come on, I won't bite.

(Reluctantly, she crosses to him. He reaches over and pulls off her sunglasses.)

Aha!

(They all react.)

Look who I found, Shirl. Our other witness. What's your name, honey?

HONEY. Honey.

AL. What are you, a parrot? I said what's your name?

HONEY. That is my name. Honey.

BUBBALOWE. Please, Mr. Feghetti, she doesn't know anything.

AL. Shut up, you lyin' double-crosser! I thought we had a deal! All this time you been pretendin' to help me out, and you been stabbin' me in the back.

BUBBALOWE. Well what do you expect me to do? She's my daughter, for God's sake!

AL. Daughter? Since when?

BUBBALOWE. Since she was born! Look, Mr. Feghetti, do what you want to me, but please – just let Honey go.

AL. No can do, Plunkett. I can't leave no witnesses. I mean, you both saw us rub Mickey out.

BUBBALOWE. But that's just it! Mickey didn't get rubbed out. He's still alive!

AL. Don't gimme that. I shot him in the heart.

BUBBALOWE. You shot him in the cigarette case! I'm telling you, he's out there somewhere, alive and well. The murder never took place, so there's nothing to take care of.

AL. Listen, I ain't bungled a hit in my entire career. When I kill a guy he stays dead. *(cocking his gun)* Now say your prayers…

HONEY. *(standing in front of* **BUBBALOWE***)* Mr. Feghetti, you can't kill my father. He didn't see anything. He wasn't even in the room!

BUBBALOWE. Honey –

AL. What are you talkin' about? Shirley chased him out through the kitchen. He even found his wallet.

BUBBALOWE. Wallet?

SHIRLEY. *(showing the wallet)* You see? Frank Plunkett.

BUBBALOWE. But you've got it all wrong. You see, I'm not Frank Plunkett –

AL. Don't play me for a chump. If you're not Frank Plunkett, then who the hell are you?

> *(**BUBBALOWE** sputters, not knowing what to say.)*

Yeah. Just what I thought. Say your prayers, Plunkett. This is the end of the road.

> *(He points his gun at **BUBBALOWE**.)*

FRANK. *(steps forward, no accent)* Wait Mr. Feghetti! You've got the wrong man. He's not Frank Plunkett. I am.

AL AND SHIRLEY AND BUBBALOWE. YOU?!!

FRANK. That's right.

AL. I thought you was Frenchie LaPoof.

FRANK. *(taking off his chef's hat)* Well, I'm not. My name's not LaPlouffe, Pagliacci, Puccini or Papadopoulos. It's Plunkett. So if that's who you want to shoot, then here I am.

AL. I don't get it – if you're Plunkett, *(turning to **BUBBALOWE**)* then who the hell are you?

BUBBALOWE. *(with a gulp)* Irving Bubbalowe.

AL. *(astounded)* You're Bubbalowe?

BUBBALOWE. Yes.

AL. Now I don't know who to shoot.

BUBBALOWE. You don't have to shoot anyone! That's what I'm trying to tell you! This has all been a terrible mistake.

AL. The only mistake you made was tryin' to steal from Alphonse Feghetti.

BUBBALOWE. But I didn't steal from you. I didn't have anything to do with it. It was Mickey's scheme from start to finish. I was just a patsy –

AL. *(pointing the gun at* **BUBBALOWE** *again)* Shut up. I don't want to hear another word. You three have been playin' me like a fiddle since I got here, and I ain't takin' it for another second! Now, *(pointing the gun)* on your knees, all of youse.

(**SHIRLEY** *cocks his gun as well.* **FRANK** *and* **HONEY** *begin to kneel.)*

(to **BUBBALOWE***)* What are you waitin' for? GET DOWN!

BUBBALOWE. No.

AL. What did you say?

BUBBALOWE. I said NO.

HONEY. *(grabbing his arm)* Pop, you'll only make things worse.

BUBBALOWE. *(losing it)* Worse? How could they possibly be worse?

HONEY. You don't want to get him upset.

BUBBALOWE. Why not? What's he going to do – kill me?

(He laughs hysterically.)

AL. What's the matter with you?

BUBBALOWE. *(pulling off his chef's hat and hurling it to the ground)* You wanna know what's the matter with me? I'll tell you what's the matter with me – when I got up this morning, the only thing on my mind was opening my restaurant. Then I find out that our friend Mickey has stashed five hundred cases of your bootleg booze in my basement, and you two show up looking to kill everybody in sight. On top of this, I've got some woman from Immigration threatening to deport my Communist French chef who turns out to be neither communist, nor French, nor my chef, for that matter; I've got the Mounties trying to arrest me for a murder I didn't commit, the Gunfight at the OK Corral playing out on my doorstep, and a neon sign I'll be paying for for the next five years lying in a million pieces on my front lawn. And what have I done to deserve all of this? Nothing! I've bent over backwards to accommodate you people! I have lied for you, I have cheated for you, I've risked being thrown in jail for you! And what do you do to thank me for all this? You stick a gun in my face and say you're going to to kill me! Alright, you want to kill me? Go right ahead. Put me out of my misery! No – you know what? I'll save you the trouble. I'll do it myself!

(He grabs **EFFING***'s gun from the bar and holds it to his temple.)*

HONEY. Pop! No!

FRANK. *(overlapping)* Mr. Bubbalowe, don't do it!

BUBBALOWE. Well??

*(***BUBBALOWE*** stands there, gun pointed at his temple, breathing heavily, a look of fierce determination on his face. A beat.* **AL** *stares at him and puffs on his unlit cigar.)*

AL. I don't know. What do you think, Shirley?

SHIRLEY. If it's an act, it's a damn good one. I think he's on the level.

(A long beat as **AL** *mulls it over.)*

AL. Yeah, I think you're right. Okay, Bubbalowe, don't do nothin' stupid. I believe you.

BUBBALOWE. You do?

AL. Yeah. I ain't gonna kill you, okay? Now put the gun down.

(A beat. Slowly **BUBBALOWE** *lowers the gun. He's about to put it down when he suddenly raises it to his temple again.)*

BUBBALOWE. What about Honey and Frank?

AL. It's okay, I ain't going to kill them neither.

BUBBALOWE. Alright.

*(***BUBBALOWE*** puts down the gun. Then quickly raises it to his temple again.)*

And Mickey?

AL. Look I ain't gonna kill nobody! I give you my word, okay?

BUBBALOWE. *(putting the gun down)* Okay.

AL. You know, Bubbalowe, you're either the bravest man I ever met – or the dumbest.

BUBBALOWE. Thank you.

AL. Come on Shirley, let's get the rest of that hooch out of here. The sooner I get outta this insane asylum the better.

*(He and **SHIRLEY** exit in to the basement. **HONEY** and **FRANK** watch them go. **BUBBALOWE** stands stock still. A beat.)*

BUBBALOWE. Are they gone?

FRANK. Yup.

BUBBALOWE. Good.

*(His knees go weak. **FRANK** catches him.)*

HONEY. *(rushing over to him)* Pop! Are you okay?

BUBBALOWE. I'm fine, I'm fine.

HONEY. That was incredible. I'm so proud of you.

FRANK. Yes, I don't know how to thank you, Mr. Bubbalowe, you saved our lives.

BUBBALOWE. Don't mention it.

HONEY. *(turning to **FRANK**)* And you too, Frank. You were so courageous, sacrificing yourself like that.

FRANK. Oh it was nothing.

HONEY. Nothing? You were wonderful.

*(She gives him a big kiss. **FRANK**'s knees go weak. **AL** and **SHIRLEY** enter from the basement carrying some boxes.)*

SHIRLEY. *(seeing the clinch)* Oh. 'Scuze us.

*(**AL** and **SHIRLEY** exit into the kitchen. **FRANK** and **HONEY** are still kissing. **BUBBALOWE** taps **FRANK** on the shoulder.)*

BUBBALOWE. Pardon me, Romeo. I hate to interrupt, but I have a bone to pick with you. What's the big idea trying to pass yourself off as François LaPlouffe?

HONEY. It wasn't his idea, Pop, it was mine. LaPlouffe's not coming.

BUBBALOWE. What?

HONEY. He found out Immigration was after him. He's on his way back to France.

BUBBALOWE. Why didn't you tell me?

HONEY. I was afraid that if you found out before the opening tonight, you would have cancelled the whole thing – and that would have been the end of Château Bubbalowe. So when Frank showed up, I asked him to take LaPlouffe's place.

BUBBALOWE. How could you do such a thing, Honey?

HONEY. Well, it's working, isn't it? Have you had a look in the kitchen lately?

BUBBALOWE. Kitchen? *(looking at his watch)* Oh my God, the dinner. Look at the time! Quick you two, if we hurry we just might be able to open this restaurant after all. *(crossing to the punch bowl and giving it to her)* Here, Honey – you better get rid of this. There's another bowl in the cooler.

*(**HONEY** starts for the kitchen.)*

On second thought, put it in the shed. We could use it for paint thinner.

(She laughs as she exits into the kitchen.)

And as for you, Mr. Plunkett –

FRANK. It's alright, Mr. Bubbalowe, I know what you're going to say. I should have been honest with you from the start. I should never have agreed to go along with this charade. I risked your life and Honey's as well as the future of your business, and it was wrong of me.

BUBBALOWE. That's right. That's exactly what I was going to say.

*(**FRANK** takes off his chef's hat and begins to look for his suitcase.)*

Oh, and one thing more –

FRANK. Yes, Mr. Bubbalowe?

BUBBALOWE. *(throwing his arms around* **FRANK***)* You're hired! Stay as long as you like!

FRANK. Oh, thank you so much, you won't regret this.

(He heads for the kitchen.)

(turning back) I'm going to prove to you I'm worth every penny of that two hundred dollars a week.

(He exits through one door as **HONEY** *enters through the other carrying the other bowl of punch.)*

BUBBALOWE. Two hun – ? Hey, just a minute!

HONEY. Pops, our guests are arriving. I just saw the mayor and his wife pull up.

BUBBALOWE. *(looks at himself)* Oh my God. I've got to get changed. Now where did I leave that jacket?

HONEY. I think it's in the closet.

(He crosses to the closet door as **AL** *and* **SHIRLEY** *enter from the kitchen. He opens the door.* **VERONICA** *steps out dressed only in her slip with a chef's hat on her head.* **AL** *whistles. Everyone stares.)*

BUBBALOWE. Miss Snook!

AL. Nice hat.

HONEY. What were you doing in there?

VERONICA. Please, I can explain –

AL. I can hardly wait.

(Suddenly, **EFFING** *stirs. Everyone turns to him.)*

EFFING. *(opening his eyes and looking around)* What's going on? Oh, my head – *(seeing* **BUBBALOWE***)* Bubbalowe! *(getting up a little shakily)* There you are. You're coming with me, mister.

VERONICA. *(to* **EFFING***)* Wait! Just a minute!

*(***EFFING** *turns to* **VERONICA***.)*

EFFING. Who are you?

VERONICA. *(crushed)* Who am I? Hammy, it's me – Nonnie! Don't you remember?

EFFING. I'm sorry, I don't think we've met.

VERONICA. What are you talking about? You're holding my dress!

*(**EFFING** looks down, sees the dress, and looks up at the others who are all staring at him. He screams and drops the dress as if it's just burned his hand.)*

EFFING. Where did that come from?

VERONICA. You tore it off me.

BUBBALOWE. He did?

EFFING. I did nothing of the kind. I've never met this woman before in my life!

AL. Oh yes you have. I seen the whole thing. *(indicating basement door)* I was right behind that door. You oughta be ashamed of yourself! A man in your position, takin' advantage of a woman in distress.

SHIRLEY. *(with a look to the dress)* She ain't in dat dress no more!

BUBBALOWE. Yes, Constable. What would your wife say?

VERONICA. Wife? You're married??

EFFING. Oh my God. Mildred!

(earnestly) I don't understand how this could have happened. It must have been that bump on the head I got when I went down the chute!

AL. Sure. Pull the other one. Do ya think they're going to buy a story like that down at headquarters?

EFFING. Please, if my Superintendent finds about this, I'll lose my promotion. He'll ship me off to Inuvik!

SHIRLEY. Inuvik? Gee, that sounds painful.

AL. Tell you what, Effing. We'll make you a deal. You forget everything that's happened here today –

EFFING. I can't do that. There's been a murder here.

VERONICA. A murder?

EFFING. That's right. A fellow by the name of Mickey McCall.

HONEY. But he's not dead, Constable.

SHIRLEY. Boy, you folks are really somethin.' When you come up with a story, you stick to it.

EFFING. What do you mean he's not dead?

(**MICKEY** *enters from the archway.*)

MICKEY. Excuse me –

HONEY. Mickey!

SHIRLEY. Holy Mother of –

AL. I don't believe it!

BUBBALOWE. Mickey! (*ushering him in*) Come on in. How nice of you to drop by.

MICKEY. Thank you. I'm sorry, have we met?

BUBBALOWE. Constable Effing, may I present Mickey McCall.

MICKEY. Pleased to meet you, Mr. McCall.

EFFING. I beg your pardon?

BUBBALOWE. He's very bad with names.

MICKEY. Can anyone tell me how to get to Niagara Falls?

BUBBALOWE. Here, sit down, Mickey. You've had a hard day. Have some punch.

(**HONEY** *pours a glass and hands it to* **MICKEY**.)

So as you can see, Constable, the rumours of Mickey McCall's murder have been greatly exaggerated.

EFFING. Perhaps so. (*pointing to the basement*) But you're still not in the clear. What about that contraband?

VERONICA. What about my dress?

EFFING. Oh, yes, er –

AL. So as I was saying, Constable. You just forget the whole thing – then we'll do the same. What do you say?

(**EFFING** *looks at* **VERONICA**, *looks at* **AL**, *sighs.*)

EFFING. Alright, it's a deal.

(**AL** *and* **EFFING** *shake.* **EFFING** *hands* **VERONICA** *what's left of her dress.*)

EFFING. *(cont.)* Miss Snook, if I did anything I should apologize for, I, well – I apologize.

VERONICA. Thank you, Constable.

BUBBALOWE. *(handing **EFFING** his hat and gun from the bar)* Give our regards to Mildred.

EFFING. Thank you. Well, I'll take my leave, then.

(He nods and exits into the closet. Beat. He comes out, straightens his uniform.)

Good evening.

(He exits through the archway with as much dignity as he can muster.)

VERONICA. *(turning to **AL**)* Thanks for coming to my rescue, Mr. Dumpty. That was very chivalrous of you.

AL. *(flattered)* Only too happy to be of service to you, Miss Shnook. *(to **SHIRLEY**)* Hey, you hear that, Shirl? I'm shiverless!

BUBBALOWE. That was some negotiation. Thanks, Mr. Feghetti.

AL. *(offering his hand, magnanimously)* Hey, call me Noodles.

BUBBALOWE. *(as they shake)* Sure – Noodles.

VERONICA. *(turning to **AL**)* Noodles? You mean you're Noodles Feghetti?

AL. Only to my very close friends.

VERONICA. I can't believe it – Noodles Feghetti the gangster? Gee, I've never met anybody famous before!

AL. *(modestly)* Aw, I ain't so special.

VERONICA. Nonsense! I read all about you in Life magazine!

AL. Well, you can't believe everything you read. My life ain't all it's cracked up to be. I mean, sometimes it can get awful lonely at the top, you know?

VERONICA. Oh, I do know!

AL. I swear, I'd give it all up in a second if I could just find the right woman – someone who appreciates me for who I am.

VERONICA. I know exactly what you mean.

AL. Say, you ever been to Chicago?

VERONICA. No, but I've always wanted to go.

AL. Well, we're headin' there in about twenty minutes. How'd you like a guided tour?

VERONICA. You mean you'd take me with you?

AL. I might as well – I'm takin' your paddy wagon.

BUBBALOWE. Alright everybody, we've got a restaurant to open here. Noodles, why don't you and Shirley get those boxes out of here.

(Unnoticed, **MICKEY** *has crossed to the gramophone and is cranking it up.)*

AL. *(smiling and taking* **VERONICA***'s hand)* Sure, Boss.

*(***AL.**, **SHIRLEY** *and* **VERONICA** *exit.)*

BUBBALOWE. Honey, get that punch into the dining room.

HONEY. OK, Pops.

BUBBALOWE. *(crossing to the kitchen and yelling through the door)* And Frank, get in here with that goose and – wait a minute – *(noticing the music)* Oh my God!

HONEY. What is it?

BUBBALOWE. Those people in there are expecting François LaPlouffe, the *singing* chef! Who's going to sing for them?

*(***MICKEY** *joins in with the record. He is a wonderful singer.* **FRANK** *enters from kitchen carrying the Goose Gallantine.)*

MICKEY. *(singing)* La-la-la-la-la –

BUBBALOWE. Mickey? *(crossing to* **MICKEY***)* You're a life-saver!

(He gives him a big kiss on the forehead.)

MICKEY. I'm sorry. I don't believe we've met.

BUBBALOWE. Sure we have. I'm Irving Bubbalowe. And you – are François LaPlouffe!

(**BUBBALOWE** *takes the Goose Gallantine from* **FRANK**, *hands it to* **MICKEY**, *takes* **FRANK**'s *hat and puts it on* **MICKEY**'s *head, and guides him toward the dining room.* **HONEY** *hands* **BUBBALOWE** *his jacket, and they all follow* **MICKEY** *into the dining room, singing the aria.*)

(*The curtain falls.*)

End of Play

PROPERTY LIST

Crash box SR for chute business (coin dropping, bottle dropping)

Phone on bar

13 boxes labelled "DOMINION WAREHOUSE" and "FRENCH
    CANADIAN PEA SOUP"

Canadian money ($20 bills, circa 1932)

10 whiskey bottles with labels (circa 1932)

Misc. bottles for box dressing

Old gramophone on bar (should work, although sound will come from
    tech.)

Tuxedo jacket on hangar (Bubbalowe, pg. 7)

Cigarette case with cigarettes (Mickey, pg. 9)

Large recipe book (Honey, pg. 11)

Chef's hat (Honey, pg. 11)

Suitcase with "FRANK PLUNKETT" printed on the side in large letters
    (Frank, pg. 13)

Punch bowl of drinkable liquid with ladle and glasses on tray (Honey,
    pg. 15)

Business cards on old card stock that read, "Frank Plunkett, Chef de
    Maîson, Maxim's (Frank, pg. 18)

Two large sacks, dressed to look heavy, for the "geese" (Bubbalowe, pg.
    20)

Cigar (Al, pg. 25)

Large coin (Shirley, pg. 27)

Briefcase (Veronica, pg. 27)

Business cards on old card stock that read, "Veronica Snook,
    Government of Canada" (Veronica, pg. 28)

"Salmon" wrapped in newspaper (Honey, pg. 30)

Wallet (Shirley, pg. 33)

Notebook and pencil (Effing, pg. 40)

Trick whiskey bottle – must open in Bubbalowe's pants (Bubbalowe, pg.
    45)

Large, absorbent rag under bar (Bubbalowe, pg. 46)

Salmon on platter (Honey, pg. 55)

Set of keys (Bubbalowe, pg. 60)

1 box labelled "DOMINION WAREHOUSE" and "CANADIAN PEA
    SOUP" with several cans inside with generic pork and beans labels
    (Effing, pg. 61)

Whiskey bottle under chef's hat worn by Al (Al, pg. 62)

Dishcloth (Honey, pg. 63, 67)

Cigarette case with bullet stuck in it (Mickey, pg. 70)

Salmon mousse – practical, mold filled with guck (Bubbalowe, pg. 74)

1 whiskey bottle under chef's hat with drinkable liquid (Al, pg. 75)

Bowl of fruit (Frank, pg. 77)

Handcuffs (Veronica, pg. 78)

Smoking saucepan (Honey, pg. 78)

10 whiskey bottles under chef's hats pre-set for Act II (Bubbalowe, pg. 83)

Boxes (Frank, pg. 84) Note: re-use Act I boxes

Bowl of fruit rigged with white napkins to fit on Honey's head (Honey, pg. 88)

Salmon mousse – practical, mold filled with guck (Frank, pg. 94)

Whiskey bottle (Effing, pg. 95)

Banana (Honey, pg. 102)

Bowl of punch (Honey, pg. 109)

Goose Gallantine on platter (Frank, pg. 114)

Restaurant Stuff
15 chef's hats
chef's coats
aprons
table cloths

Storage Closet
Canned goods
Assorted linens
12 wooden hangars

Guns
One each for Mickey, Shirley and Effing
One practical gun for Al

Boxes
Box 1: sealed, with bottles

Box 2: sealed, with bottles

Box 3: open, with bottles (one of which is removed but not opened)

Box 4: sealed, with bottles

Box 5: open, with bottles (one of which is removed but not opened)

Box 6: open, with bottles (one of which is removed but not opened)

Box 7: open, with bottles (including Bubbalowe's trick bottle with liquid)

Box 8: dressed with cans of pork and beans

Box 9: sealed, with bottles

Box 10: sealed, with bottles

Bottles
Bubbalowe's trick bottle (from Box #7)

Al's bottle that he tucks into his chef's jacket in the closet. It is empty in Act I but should be replaced at intermission for a bottle with liquid in it.

10 bottles under chef's hats in the closet (pre-set at intermission); two must have liquid: one which Al gets from the closet (pg. 75), the other that Bubbalowe forgets to pack into the case later

1 bottle with liquid that Effing brings from the basement (no cork) (pg. 95)

COSTUME PLOT

IRVING BUBBALOWE
Grey pants with elastic waistband
Striped shirt
Suspenders
Sock garters
Patterned socks
Patterned boxer shorts
Patterned tie
Black shoes
Dark blue jacket
Black tuxedo pants
Black tuxedo jacket

MICKEY MCCALL
Tan work boots
White socks
Plaid boxer shorts
Blue overalls with "Dominion Warehouse" stencilled on back
Tan shirt, Mandarin collar
Red kerchief
Tan ball cap

HONEY BUBBALOWE
Patterned dress with belt
Dark brown pumps
Dark brown overcoat
Dark brown hat
Brown purse
Red velvet dress
Black pumps
Black bead necklace
Red sunglasses with diamante trim
Watch
White chef's hat
White chef's jacket
White chef's jacket with dirt on front

FRANK PLUNKETT
Black shoes
Black socks
Black dress pants
Patterned sports jacket
Bow tie
Tan dress shirt
Suspenders

Tan vest
Tan fedora
Watch
Cook's jacket with Velcro closure
Cook's jacket with button closure
Chef's hat
Black tuxedo jacket, at least one size larger than normal

ALFONSE FEGHETTI
Black wing-tip shoes
Black suit pants with stripes
Black suit jacket with stripes
Red flower for buttonhole
Kerchief in breast pocket
Dress shirt
Maroon tie
Black fedora
Over-the-shoulder gun holster
Suspenders
Black socks
Large ring
Watch
White chef's hat
White chef's jacket

SHIRLEY
Black shoes
Black suit pants with stripes
Black suit jacket with stripes
Black dress shirt
White tie
Suspenders
Over-the-shoulder gun holster
Grey kerchief in breast pocket
Black fedora
Watch
White chef's hat
White chef's jacket

CONSTABLE EFFING
Mountie dress uniform – (Black knee-high boots, dark blue jodhpurs
    with yellow stripe, red serge coat with brass buttons and trim)
White socks
Torn red serge coat, broken down and stained
Torn, broken down dark blue jodhpurs
Brown Mountie hat
Brown Mountie hat with hole in top
Black Sam Brown belt with gun holster
Kneepads

VERONICA SNOOK
Black pumps
Black slip
Black bra
Patterned dress with tie in back
Overcoat
Black tam
Tortoiseshell glasses
Watch
Black bead necklace
Patterned dress (same as above) with tear-away snaps in back, ripped
One heel-less black pump
White chef's hat

Stairs to 2nd floor

Archway

Chute

Barstools

Bar

Stairs to basement

Doors to kitchen

Doors to dining room

Closet

Chairs

Table

* Image appears courtesy of the authors